I0607556

Wicked Distractions

WICKED GAMES

ANGELA ADDAMS

Wicked Games
ISBN # 978-1-80250-562-7
©Copyright Angela Addams 2023
Cover Art by Kelly Martin ©Copyright August 2023
Interior text design by Claire Siemaszkiewicz
Totally Bound Publishing

WICKED GAMES

Dedication

Dedicated to my own hardworking ass.

Chapter One

Elena had grown up like a princess, but now she was a queen. The queen of fun and games—and the room full of staggeringly wealthy players were getting exactly what they paid for.

"Blindfolds off, gentlemen." She'd been herding the crowd of millionaires through the maze with the threat of her long whip while the other Kitty Cats had been using their own torture devices of choice. The men were sweaty, lash-streaked and panting for more. All were big-shot bankers, lawyers, CEOs of this and that who sure loved to play tag and seemed to truly enjoy the chase, 'be chased' model that Elena had developed.

As they took off their blindfolds, the men surveyed the Kitty Cats with their hungry lust-filled eyes, greedily gorging on the feast of flesh before them. The Cats all stood with kink tools in hand, looking glamorous in their rhinestones and sequined skirts and halters. The men were no doubt wondering who had paddled them so soundly, which of the sly Cats had whipped with such precision. It obviously was a fun guessing game if the expressions held true, an added bonus of mystery and intrigue, and the men all looked eager to get on with more fun.

Perfectly primed for an upsell. Just as Elena had intended.

"Look around you, sirs," Elena said as she flourished her whip, giving a little snap to remind them who was in charge. "My mistresses of pain are here for your pleasure, but only if you're willing to pay for their time. Make your choices and be quick about it. The mistresses are busy."

Speaking of which, Elena was definitely pushing her luck, timewise. She had an eight-p.m. flight to catch and was already running late.

"Use your wristbands to upgrade your package, and you'll find the surprises will keep coming all night long."

The electronic wristbands had been her idea, pitched at last month's department meeting. She watched as the men scrambled to their favorite Kitty Cat then raised their wrists to swipe along the small devices the girls all had. It was an ingenious way to collect money that gave the men very little time to regret the hefty prices they'd find on their bank statements later.

It was well worth the cost, if you asked her. The Kitty Cats were all trained for whatever kind of fun the men wanted, and everyone would leave very satisfied. Even still, to the uninitiated, that first whopper of an upsell sometimes came with some sticker shock. She'd fielded a few angrily whispered phone calls over the last few weeks, the men always seeking discretion, and had handled them all with grace and, ironically, another upsell on something the men just couldn't live without. Sabine had been delighted, and Elena knew a promotion was now within her grasp.

Which was why she, along with a group of high-achieving Kitty Cat colleagues, had all been invited to a private getaway for rest, relaxation and a whole lot of competitive fun by their esteemed boss, Sabine Cowan. Elena was pumped to be going on the exclusive trip. Yes, it happened to fall over Christmas, and yes, normally Elena would be spending that day and the ones around it working at a foodbank or soup kitchen, but she figured that this year, and only this year, she'd set aside her lifelong quest for redemption and indulge herself. Not only that, but this was the perfect opportunity for Elena to tempt Sabine on a few ideas that Elena had, not to mention a proposal for a promotion that would hoist her into the upper echelon of Cowan Enterprises in one fell swoop. Elena wanted her 'queen of games' status to be the real deal, and this trip was one step closer to making it happen.

Yes, Sabine had said this was a no-business kind of trip and work phones were to be left at headquarters, but Elena figured being the only single traveler on the trip, Sabine might take pity on her and let her be a third wheel with her and her partner, Trent, where inevitably business might come up in conversation.

It will definitely come up. The other Cats on the trip might be content to wait for their boss to handpick them for a new job or a raise, but Elena had other plans. She was always ready for opportunities that might come knocking…or ones that she set up accidentally on purpose so she'd pull ahead of the high-achieving pack of Cats.

It wasn't cheating if she wasn't going for the same raise everyone else was. Her proposal would be for a new position, not yet occupied by anyone in the company.

The fact that Elena didn't have a plus one suited her just fine...mostly. Really, it was no big deal that she would be attending the getaway alone when all the other Cats would be bringing significant or not-so-significant others with them. Her only friends were the ones she worked with, and spending time with them on a tropical island for the holidays was just as appealing as spending it with a non-existent boyfriend.

At least, that's what she was telling herself. Of course, it would be nice to walk along the beach at dusk, holding hands and being all romantic with someone, but it would also be nice to stretch out on a queen-size bed and not have to compromise on activities. Also, once her plan was in play, she was determined to get Sabine talking shop, something that Elena felt would be better achieved if she were alone.

"Ladies, I'm out of here," Elena said to the two Kitty Cats managing the organization of the partner-pairing that was underway. "If there are any problems, call Anthony."

"You got it, boss," Sapphire said with a wink. "Have fun!"

Sapphire had gone on the trip the previous year and raved to anyone who would listen that it was not to be missed. The only reason she couldn't go this year was because she was booked for two weeks with one of her sugar-daddy clients, and she'd be wined, dined and fucked to her heart's content. It had been Sapphire who'd told Elena that this trip was a must-do if she wanted private time to talk to Sabine. It was hard enough to track the woman down day to day, she was so busy, and this trip would give her plenty of free time on a secluded island. What better way to hijack a tanning session for some idea sharing and promotion wheeling and dealing?

Elena did a quick wardrobe change, because skintight latex bodysuits were not all that practical for lounging on a private jet. Instead, she slipped on yoga pants and a tank under her bulky sweater. It was cold as shit in New York, but she wanted to be able to shed the layers once she was airborne and on her way to the Bahamas.

She took an Uber to the airport and got slightly turned around once inside, looking for the gate that would take her to Cowan Enterprises private jet. It wasn't every day that someone got an invite to travel in luxury, and finding where she needed to be was made more confusing by the sheer number of travelers departing. Holiday season was chaos! She had to wonder why anyone would do this every year just to visit family. Although, she did have a very skewed set of principles when it came to wanting to spend time with hers. She definitely wouldn't travel to see anyone related to her at any point in her adult life.

She wasn't a black sheep...far from it. She was the white sheep among wolves, and she'd rather be bitten by fire ants than have to spend the holidays with her father.

She was just about to text a distress, hopelessly lost plea to Adam Lancaster, head of Cowan security, when she was swept up in a sprinting mob, their panic palpable as they raced to a connecting flight. She didn't know where they were headed destination-wise, but she could tell by their frantic shouts that they absolutely couldn't miss the flight.

Her hair was yanked in one direction, her bag in another. She teetered on her fashionable but maybe not practical heels and cursed herself for getting caught up in a tornado of bodies. If she hit the floor, she'd be trampled for sure.

Wonderful, death by frantic holiday traveler stampede.

She reached a hand out, trying to force her way through the crowd by parting the rushing people next to her, when a firm grip latched onto her outstretched fingers. Before she could tumble back any farther, she was wrenched from the melee, wrapped in strong arms and moved out of the way, dragging her small carryon bag with her. As she began to catch her breath, whoever was holding her kept walking, practically carrying her toward the side of the main walkway.

"I'm good," she gasped, clasping her hands for a hold on the stranger's arms, her feet unsteady as she tripped along with him. "You can put me down now."

Except the person didn't put her down. In fact, he — and it was definitely a massively muscled he — seemed to be ignoring her as he swiftly moved her down a short side hallway.

"Hey! I said, I'm fine. Let me go!"

"Hush." He clamped his hand over her mouth, sending her straight into ballistic mode.

She wrenched her body, dropping her weight to hang like a limp noodle, no longer cooperating with him as she dug her heels into the carpet.

It didn't slow him down at all.

She scratched her nails between his fingers, digging in so she was sure she was drawing blood.

Again, no impact.

She swung her bag around and heaved her leg up, striking backward, aiming for a knee, shin, whatever she could hit with her spiky heels as her bag connected with the side of his face.

"Ouch, shit!"

That gravelly voice rolled over her, down her spine, zapping every synapsis she had and waking up the dormant desires she kept hidden.

"Princess, it's me." He spun her around then pushed her up against the wall. He wasn't being rough, though she wished he would be. His face was the same as it had always been—rugged, a scruffy jaw, a scar that he'd earned on her behalf bisecting his cheek, hazel eyes rimmed by dark lashes. He'd grown his hair out from his usual military cut so it hung in soft waves like dark ribbons of chocolate. Her breath left her lungs, suctioned out by shock. "It's me, Elena."

"I know it's you." She didn't, of course, not at first, but his voice...*oh fuck*...that voice haunted her most sinful dreams. That voice was enough to melt her panties and set her heart on fire.

That voice belonged to *Rylan Ward*.

The love of her life.

The man of her dreams.

The stubborn ass who always put duty over his heart and social etiquette over his desire.

She kneed him in the nuts then pushed him backward as he started to fall, a moan slipping from his clenched lips.

"And I told you never to ambush me like that." In fact, she'd told him she never wanted to see him again, which, at the time, had been a big fat lie that he had taken as truth. It'd been three years since they'd last spoken.

"Princess, you're in danger," he gasped from the ground, panting through his pain as he shifted into a crouch, already recovering from her cheap shot.

Of course, she should have known he had balls of steel.

"Stop calling me that. I'm *not* a princess." If she'd ever been one to begin with... Her family had been royals by coup, generations of politics, of taking what didn't belong to them, of getting their way if only because of their surname, until it had all come crashing down around them.

"I have to get you to safety." Ry uncurled himself, slowly rising to his full height to tower over Elena. He was all muscle and sinew under his black suit and white shirt, his tie so tight to his throat that he moved when he swallowed. "There are men—"

"I told you before… I don't want protection from you."

He grabbed her arm, and she tugged it back. Their eyes locked like magnets, hers shooting daggers, his narrowed and piercing.

"And I told you that I'd never put you in danger." He flinched, and in an instant, Elena knew he'd failed at least one of his missions.

"Cai is dead, isn't he?"

Ry gulped, his Adam's apple bobbing. "Last night."

Her world tilted, and this time when he gripped her arm, she didn't fight him off. Her father, Cai Russio, was a very bad man with many sins on his shoulders. She hated him for who he was, what he stood for, what he'd demanded from everyone, but he was still her father—the last of her blood relations, actually.

"Cancer. He didn't want anyone to know. It took him fast." Ry was blunt, but she could hear the war behind his words. They both knew that her father deserved a worse death than that. True to his nature, though, Ry had protected the man until his last breath. "They'll come for you now that he's gone."

Her father, the enemy of her heart, her soul, her conscience, had been the catalyst behind a lot of people wanting the Russio family dead…including Elena. There had always been a price on his head, but he had been legendary in his ruthlessness and cunning in his ability to disappear. No hitman or woman ever got to him, mostly thanks to Ry.

Ironic that it was cancer that did the job in the end, free of charge.

Now it was Elena's turn to gulp, forcefully pushing down the boulder growing in her throat. "Where will you take me?"

He swayed closer, his focus straying to her lips then down her throat before sliding back to meet her gaze. She raised her hand to trace his scar, the divot along his flesh a familiar track, but held back at the last second, curling her fingers instead. Touching Ry would be a mistake. It would always be a mistake. She tilted her head up anyway, brushing her body against his and felt his grip loosen, like he was giving in, finally accepting that he wanted her as much as she wanted him.

"Somewhere safe," he said, his gravelly voice hushed.

She so badly wished this to be under different circumstances. For years, she'd fantasized about Ry coming to sweep her away—to confess his undying love, or hell, even just admitting to his lust, and taking her off to a private island where they could be alone together.

Reality hit Elena upside the head. He wasn't here for that. He was here to destroy her plans.

"I'm headed to a secluded place. I'll be safe there. Security will—"

"No," Ry growled. "I have a place we'll go. Come on. We're wasting time."

He tightened his grip on her arm as the wall he always put between them rose up to shutter his feelings once again. She wrenched her arm, doing nothing to loosen his grip.

"Don't start this shit again, Elena. We don't have time—"

"Everything okay here, Elena?"

Elena turned her head, snapping herself away from Ry's hard eyes to see Adam, his arms crossed, eyes narrowed, chin up. He was a brick warehouse where Ry was more like a sleek mansion. A fight between the two would be disastrous, especially considering that Ry was a trained assassin, deadly in more ways than she could count.

Ry opened his mouth, and she knew what he was about to say would end up in a mess, so she beat him to it by hoisting herself up on tiptoes then planting a kiss on his cheek, startling him from saying a word.

"Everything's amazing, Adam." She yanked a stunned Ry, his arm halfway to his cheek like he could brush away her kiss, so he was facing Adam, her smile electric and, she hoped, convincing. "I'd like to introduce you to my plus one."

"Your plus one?" both men said with different tones, Adam's skeptical and Ry's full-on what-the-fuck?

"Yes, Adam Lancaster, this is Rylan Ward, my fiancé."

Chapter Two

Rylan was always in control, always thinking five steps ahead. But this...*situation* had taken a deep left turn that had him sweating beneath his suit. He'd forgotten how spicy Elena could be. She was all habanero — small, delicious-looking, so enticing that she had you thinking you wanted a taste, only to find out that she'd sear you right down to your core.

Elena kept talking, leaving Rylan behind in total shock for thirty seconds too, long to stop her from spinning her lies into irreversible truths.

Damn this woman!

"Come on, Ry. Be a gentleman, and shake Adam's hand." Elena dug her nails into his sleeve, pinching his skin as she steered his hand forward. "If he doesn't approve you on the guest list, you're not getting on the plane with me." She leaned closer to whisper, "And I know you don't want me going anywhere without you."

He cleared his throat, reassessed the situation as it was, then offered his hand. "Sorry. Got caught off guard there."

"We haven't seen each other in a long time." Elena giggled like this was all a game to her. "I distracted him."

"I take it that doesn't happen often." Adam's handshake was as firm as Rylan would expect from a guy as big and commanding as he was. "Getting easily distracted, that is."

Rylan let his comment pass with only a nod and motioned for them to move out of the hallway where they were starting to attract attention. "Where is it we're headed?"

"Bahamas, Cowan Island."

"I take it that's an invite-only location?" He knew some of the off-the-beaten-track islands in the Bahamas, and Cowan didn't sound like any he'd heard of before.

"Yep, which means we'll do a thorough background check before you're cleared to board the jet." Adam glanced at him, one eyebrow cocked. "That going to be a problem?"

Rylan shook his head. "Nah, security check will come back clean." Because it was washed and dried with a full fake background for just this kind of situation.

"Excellent," Adam said with another glance at Elena. "You've been keeping this secret tight to your chest, eh, El?"

"Ry didn't approve of my career choice," Elena said with a purr as she sidled up next to him, slipping her arm through his, her breasts pressed against his forearm. "He's finally come around to it."

Not entirely true. Rylan had no problem with her career choice, not *much* of a problem anyway. She was a grown-ass woman who could make decisions for herself. But he let the lie go because what was he going to say? *I was protecting her filthy-as-shit father for the last three years as my contract and duty demanded?*

Her strawberry-scented hair made Rylan's body come alive in ways he didn't want to ever admit. Just like how her body, pressed against his, made him flush with a possessive need that was completely inappropriate for someone of his age and purpose. Elena was, had always been, off limits.

"Just in time for the holidays," Adam said with a grin. "Sabine'll love the romance of that. I suspect you're about to get a room upgrade."

Elena squeezed his arm before hoisting herself up on tiptoes to brush a kiss against his jaw. "Hear that, honey? A room upgrade!"

Her teasing tone rankled, and Rylan wanted to chastise her like he would have when she was a teenager. This was no game. Her life was in danger.

Instead, he sighed, rubbing his hand over his face. She was too wily for his words of caution then and she hadn't changed in their time apart—other than, of course, that somehow, she'd become more beautiful, more sultry, more everything, and that was bad news for him, his dick and his integrity.

Adam led them to an offshoot of the main airport then left them in a room while he went to get security sorted.

Rylan checked for cameras, mics, anything that would suggest they weren't alone before speaking. Elena leaned against the wall, her arms crossed, breasts nearly busting out of her low-cut sweater and with a wry smirk on her face.

"This isn't going to happen your way, Elena." He tried for stern, only to see her lips curl in the sly grin he knew so well.

"It's funny that you think you have any say in my life." Elena pushed herself off the wall then sauntered to the table. She perched herself on the edge, crossing her legs at the ankle, showcasing her hourglass frame as she positioned her arms under her breasts once again, pushing her cleavage higher. She knew her assets and how to use them. If he'd been any other man, he'd be drooling, falling all over himself...and her. That's why, back when she'd been twenty, he'd been not totally cool about her joining the ranks of Sabine Cowan's Kitty Cats. He knew how other men worked. They had no self-control. But again, it wasn't his place to make those decisions, and he'd never get in the way of Elena's dreams. He didn't blame her for wanting to escape her father's control.

Right now, Ry was desperately trying not to break into a sweat. Her body on display made his clothes feel tight and the room too hot. She wasn't going to make this easy...not that he thought she would.

Rylan's mouth was dry, his collar itchy. He fought with everything he had to keep his hands at his sides as he tore his eyes away from her chest to survey the room...again. Four white walls. One table. Two chairs. Elena leaning precariously, tits on display, hips begging for hands to keep her steady, her long legs encased in skintight leggings that accentuated her right down to the impossible heels that made his dick hard.

Stop thinking about fucking her. Get your mind out of the gutter. This is a job. Your only job now.

"You trying to talk yourself out of your feelings again, Ry?" Elena sighed like he was a huge disappointment. "Always denying your needs. Some things never change, I guess."

"Be reasonable. This isn't a game." He met her eyes again, only to see the playfulness gone, replaced by something darker. "We can't go on vacation. We can't ignore the danger. There are men who want to kill you."

"Did he suffer at least?" Her topic shift didn't jar him. He knew where her mind was, where it would always be. "Did he pay for his sins?"

Rylan had worked for Elena's family since he was a young man. He'd been groomed to be ruthless in his protection of Elena's father, Cai, and, at times, by proxy, in protection of Elena as well. As loyal as he had been, if only because he had secrets of his own to keep that Cai constantly reminded him of, he knew the man was heartless, evil and that Elena had every reason to hate him.

Rylan was never asked to do anything but protect, but that didn't mean he was oblivious to the corruption that went on behind the doors he was watching or that the man he was protecting didn't deserve what he'd got in the end. He deserved much, much worse.

"It was a clean death, from what I've heard — hospice, nurses, drugs. He knew what was coming, made peace with it." Rylan carried no guilt for not being there until the bitter end. Cai had asked him to leave, to find Elena, take her away, keep her safe. It was meant to be his last job before finally being freed from any contractual obligation he had to Cai, almost ten years' worth. "He sent me to protect you because you're in danger. You're the only one left, Elena."

The only one left in the vast and treacherous Russio clan. It was hard to fathom, but it was true.

She hadn't adopted a fake identity when she'd come to work for Sabine Cowan, not like he'd have wanted, other than taking her grandmother's maiden name, Sasser. It was a name, she'd claimed, had no blood on it and no ties to the Russio clan, other than her grandmother's unfortunate run in with her grandfather who'd impregnated her, taken her child—Elena's father—then left her to die of heartbreak. Rylan had known she would never back down on her career path and her desire to work for Sabine Cowan, so he'd done his due diligence and checked out Cowan Enterprises from top to bottom. He'd been satisfied that she'd be safe with Adam and his team.

The guys who wanted to kill her father would find her, though, no matter how good Adam's security was. They would torture her for information that she didn't have. They would assassinate her, just like they'd done to her stepmother and, not for lack of trying, never succeeded with her father. They had gotten her cousins, and aunts, uncles and anyone who had ties to the Russio clan. The jury was still out on whether or not that included Rylan.

He wouldn't let that happen. *No.* He would die before he let them near her. In fact, death would be a welcomed end game for him once he completed his mission, because while he may not have actively participated in Cai's shit, he certainly never stopped it from happening. Anyone who associated with the Russio's was dirty…everyone except Elena.

She was innocent and didn't deserve to carry the burden of her family's sins.

"I don't want protection." *From you* went without saying. She'd always been resistant to Rylan watching out for her. She'd wanted freedom. She'd wanted independence. And now that she had it, he was going to take it away — at least until he could ensure she was safe.

"I know you're not hearing me, Ry." She pushed herself off the table then got all up in Rylan's space. "I. Don't. Want. Your. Kind. Of. Protection." Her eyes were on fire, her chest heaving from pent-up rage that he could practically see emanating from her. It was enough to make him step back, knowing that she was just as likely to nail him in the balls as she was to kiss him. And he couldn't let either of those things happen again.

"Too bad," he snapped, attempting to take back control. "This isn't your decision right now. You're being reckless and naïve. You may not want me to call you princess but you're acting like one."

She flinched, and he regretted his words but he didn't take them back. Her father had insisted everyone call her Princess Elena, not because she was royalty but because she was destined to inherit his throne. And therein lay the biggest problem for Elena. She held the proverbial keys to his fortune, a fortune that had been built in blood. Cai's enemies wanted it, and they thought Elena would know how to access it. She didn't — not yet, anyway — but she would, and that was all her father's enemies needed to rest their hopes on.

"I've been doing fine on my own." Her words are clipped, edged with warning but Rylan held his ground. "I'm alive, aren't I?"

"You won't be if these guys catch up with you." He leaned forward, using his height and weight to loom. "And they *will* catch up with you, it's only a matter of time. We have to go into hiding."

"No."

"Elena —"

"No!" She broke away from him to pace to the other side of the room. "No! I won't run. I won't leave my life." When she turned to face him, he saw a vulnerability that he'd only ever seen once before. "I've built something here, Ry." She lifted her hands. "I have a life and friends. People give a shit about me here. I won't disappear on them. I won't leave them wondering what happened to me." She scoffed. "And really, I don't think they'd let me, either. Adam would send out search parties. Trent would use his influence to track me down. Sabine would —"

"They wouldn't find us," Rylan said softly, knowing they'd tread into sensitive territory. He didn't want to take away her freedom or her happiness, but he didn't want her to die because of it, either. "You know they won't." Elena was well aware of the contingency plan if the shit hit the fan. She knew that where he was going to take her, no one would find them. It's where he should have taken Cai, but the old man wanted nothing to do with the place. He wanted to die in luxury, which meant a hell of a lot of guarding. In the end, though, he got his wish, a giant 'fuck you' to the hitmen who'd been circling like sharks. He'd died on his own terms.

She sighed, lowered her hands, her shoulders slumping. "Yeah, I know." When she looked up at him again, she was soft around the edges. "Don't do this to me. My life is finally normal. Please, Ry, if you can keep me safe somewhere else, you can keep me safe on an island, too."

They both knew that wasn't true.

All the same, her uncharacteristic begging was a knife to the heart.

"I haven't had time to assess the island's vulnerabilities," he said, his mind working all the angles, knowing that her pleading was not something she did on a whim. "I don't know if it's secure."

"You let me come here in the first place...to work for Cowan Enterprises." As if he'd had a choice. She'd set her mind on it, so he made sure it would work. Ultimately though, it was her father who let her go. "If anything, security has only gotten better." She waved her arm, making her bracelets clank. "We all wear GPS trackers. Adam can find us anywhere we want him to."

Which was how he must have found them in the airport. Smart thinking, although it concerned Rylan as to why Adam would find the need to be able to track the employees in that way. Did it mean they were often in danger?

"Wipe that worried look off your face, Ry." Elena rolled her eyes. "It's not mandatory to wear the GPS." She clinked her bracelets again, letting him know exactly where the tracker was located. "But I could practically hear your voice in my head when Adam offered it. I knew you'd approve if security had my whereabouts at all times."

She crossed the room to stand in front of him, looking at him through her long, dark eyelashes. "Don't take this away from me," she said again as she slipped her arms around his waist. "Please, Ry. Let me have this. You told me to find normal, and I did. I found it. I love it. We'll be safe."

"Elena," he groaned. He was stiff, on alert, her body so close, making every warning-light go off in his head.

"You know you want to..." She tilted her face up as she let her words trail off, unspoken needs hanging between them.

She'd always made it clear that she was attracted to him, and he'd always been equally clear that he wouldn't cross that boundary. Obligation to her father, a sense of duty, their age gap, all of it made the decision easier back then. Now…well…his body wasn't getting the memo that she was still off limits. His mind gave him traitorous what-ifs and he knew, if he gave in, he'd be lost to it…to her.

She didn't need him in her life like that. He was dark and dangerous, rough around the edges, not fit for the woman Elena had become. She said she didn't want the title of princess anymore but to him she would always be a level above him — too good for someone like Rylan, whether she saw it that way or not. Besides, his endgame wouldn't allow it. His job was nearly over, and his future would likely come to an abrupt stop once she was safe. Too many sins in his past, too. He didn't have a hit on his head like she did, but there were a lot of guys who'd be happier if he were out of the picture for good.

Even so, he couldn't help lifting his hand to sweep away the strands of her hair that clung to her cheek then let his fingers linger against her jaw. What he wouldn't give for things to be different.

The door opened and Adam came in. "Sorry to interrupt."

Elena took a step back but slid her fingers along his until they were entwined. "We good? Did Ry pass the test?" She was teasing again, her eyes flirtatious.

A jolt of unreasonable jealousy lashed through Rylan. He wanted her to look at him like that, not Adam — not any other man, in fact. And that feeling was damn confusing.

"All clear. Glad to see you're in the security field. Never hurts to have another trained guy on the island." Adam nodded. "Time to board."

Rylan felt Elena's eyes on him, a decision taut between them.

He *had* told her to find normal and, in her own way, she had. So, it was up to him to see this through her way.

"I hope there's somewhere to get clothes. I didn't pack for a beach vacation." He hadn't packed at all. Where they'd been headed was already fully stocked.

By the squeeze of Elena's fingers, Rylan knew he might be making her happy, but he was also heading into uncertain territory in more ways than one and she was misreading it all.

Chapter Three

"Fiancé?" Ry grumbled after they were seated side-by-side in their plush lounge chairs waiting for takeoff. "You couldn't come up with something with fewer expectations?"

She loved it when he pouted. Not that anyone who didn't know him could tell, he was so stoic, but she knew.

"No, I couldn't." She leaned closer, pushing her tits along the armrest between them, knowing she was making him squirm by how much faster his finger tapped his knee. "Besides, I did ask you to marry me that one time."

"You were fifteen," he growled.

Sure, the first time she met Rylan, she'd been a very boy-crazy fifteen, had taken in his military-style buzz cut, his high cheekbones, square jaw and broad shoulders and she'd only had one thought, *I'm going to marry that man.* Of course, because she'd been fifteen, she'd blurted those words out loud, which had gotten her a bellowing chortle from her pig father and a deeper frown from Ry.

"Mr. Ward is below your station, Princess," her father had said. *"But if you're ready to be a child bride, I have plenty of friends who'd kill to pop your cherry."*

Her cheeks had nearly caught flames she'd been so embarrassed.

It had been the one and only time that her stepmother, a mere five years her elder, had stepped in to chastise her father publicly, and he'd begged off that it was all a joke. It didn't endear her more to her stepmom, but it did make her feel obligated to be a little less snarky toward the woman.

Elena had been horrified by it all. Her father had been notorious for his grotesque sense of humor, but she hadn't forgotten how Ry's expression had hardened, his eyes steady and glaring at her father like he had no fear of the man. It was the first time in her life that she'd seen anyone dare to look at Cai Russio with such disdain.

Ry had been twenty-five, brand new to the fold, and suddenly a hero in her eyes.

She had tried to do everything she could to get in Ry's way. She'd stare and drool, flirt and be completely inappropriate. He'd never once given her the time of day. She'd thought he didn't even know she existed beyond being the daughter of her boss, and she hadn't time to feast on him for long before her father had sent him on different security jobs for high-ranking members of the family. Training, he'd said. Really, Elena felt it was punishment. Her eye candy was gone. She hadn't seen Ry for more than a few minutes at a time, passing through with relatives, a brief hello, goodbye and whatever else Elena could slip in to make sure he knew what she was offering. That all changed when she turned nineteen and the circumstances unfolded in a very opportunistic way.

"Trust me. This is the easiest way to explain you being here, and it's one that everyone will buy. I've been telling the Cats for years that I have a secret fiancé." She glanced over her shoulder, sensing the current of excitement changing as Sabine Cowan herself boarded the plane. "They've been dying to meet you."

She'd used the fiancé excuse as her out for getting involved with some of the above and beyond jobs that the Kitty Cats did. She'd had no interest in participating in the escort side of Cowan Enterprises. It wasn't her thing. She was more of a 'look but don't touch' kind of woman and enjoyed planning games more than participating in them with clients. She hadn't known when she'd first started working for Sabine Cowan that it had always been her own choice, and she hadn't needed a ruse to opt out of some of the job descriptions. If she didn't want to escort, she didn't have to — no pressure, no expectation, no guilt. Despite that, she'd kept up the fiancé excuse, mainly because it made her happy to fantasize about one day being with Ry for real.

Ry frowned at her, his lips opening, no doubt to question her, but she lifted her fingers to her lips to shush him just as Sabine swept down the aisle.

"Welcome everyone!" Sabine said with a huge grin. "I'm so happy you're all able to join us for this much-deserved vacation." She touched Elena's shoulder as she moved past their seats. "And I want to especially welcome all of the significant others who have agreed to give up family traditions to create one with us, Kitty Cat style." She winked at Elena then spun to face the others. "We're going to get going shortly. Please stay seated with your belts on until the pilot gives the all-clear. Once we're good, you can explore the jet and take advantage of the amenities...all of them. Couples massage is in the master suite."

A titter of *ohhs* and *ahhs* went through the length of the seating area. There were twenty Cats and partners in total, plus Sabine, her partner Trent, Adam and his girlfriend Missy, along with five more security guys.

"Mind if we sit here?" Sabine swooped into the seats across from Elena and Ry, Trent in tow.

This was a dream come true just on its own. Elena sat up straighter, her spine snapped to attention. To have her esteemed boss asking to join her for the three-hour flight? *Hell yes!*

Except...now that Ry was with her, she couldn't use the opportunity to pick her boss's brain about business stuff or share her ideas for a few new games and tournaments she'd planned. She'd have to play along with the ruse she'd started because, for sure, Sabine would want to get to know her fiancé.

Damn it!

Her only goal on this trip had been to position herself so that she could discuss a promotion with Sabine. The implications of having Ry along hit her like a sledgehammer, and she slumped back into the plush leather. He was there as her protection... What if her hunters did manage to track her down? On Sabine's private island? Then what? There'd be a scene—a major situation, probably. Everyone would find out who she really was. Her carefully constructed life would crumble, not to mention that she could actually be murdered.

She gave herself a mental slap.

No chance of that happening. Adam had security covered. He always thought of every angle, even ones he didn't know about, like assassins coming to take out the last living member of the Russio family. He was solid…dependable, just like Ry.

She fully believed that they'd both keep her safe.

She'd have to play this game now…the one where Ry was her long-lost fiancé, not her father's deathbed sworn protector. Otherwise, she might as well tell Sabine her sordid history and confess who her father had been. *A despicable monster.*

Sabine would likely fire her on the spot. Who would want someone with that kind of baggage in her company?

Everything she'd worked her ass for would be lost.

Dread pooled in her gut, and she laid her hand across her belly. Throwing up all over Sabine wouldn't go over well, either.

Get your shit together, girl!

The fact remained that Sabine took security and privacy very seriously. So seriously that if she found out Elena had lied, well, Elena's future prospects at Cowan Enterprises would be nonexistent. Loyalty was a verb and lying a fireable offense. A lump the size of a bolder settled in Elena's throat, and no amount of water would dislodge it.

"Ms. Cowan, champagne is on ice and drinks will be served once we're in the air," a server said as she leaned toward Sabine.

"Thanks, Kass. That'll be fine." Sabine turned her wide smile to Ry, catching him in her crosshairs, confirming to Elena that he was the reason Sabine had sat down across from them in the first place.

Alarm bells went off in Elena's head, giving her an instant headache. She could only hope that Ry would pass Sabine's interrogation.

"You must be Rylan Ward, our late addition to the party." Sabine tapped her long nails against the leather seat, not in the irritated way that Ry had been drilling his knee but in a way that reminded Elena of a cat testing its claws.

"Sorry for dropping him on you like this, Sabine," Elena blurted, heat lacing up her throat to her cheeks. "Ry has a schedule that always made it hard to plan."

"No worries at all, El." Sabine swept her gaze to Elena with a Cheshire grin that did nothing to dispel Elena's anxiety. "You've talked about your mysterious man for a long time, and we're happy to have him join us."

She *had* talked about Ry a lot, so much so that her blush was more for him learning that now than Sabine's focused attention.

"Yes, thank you for allowing me on board. I was ready to sweep El away, carry her over my shoulder if I had to. I know she's a workaholic."

And now Elena was envisioning Ry hoisting her over his shoulder, a hand on her ass, her tits pressed against his back. *Sheesh! This man!* Anxiety was effectively obliterated by the distracting image. The thought of him hoisting her up his body, tearing her away so he could ravish her…? *Mmmmm, yes.*

"Aren't we all?" Sabine said, effectively popping Elena's fantasy bubble.

Ry chuckled, a noise Elena wasn't sure she'd ever heard come out of him. "Adam said my security check was clean."

"And it was, it was." Sabine steepled her fingers, her legs crossed as she leaned forward slightly, definitely intrigued. "I'm curious about you, though. Can't blame me really, can you? Elena has been a major player in my company for years. She's worked her way up with steady grace. In fact, this trip is a reward for all her hard work. Yet, this is the first time we're meeting you. Why is that?"

"We had a fight," Elena blurted before Ry could respond. "He didn't approve—"

"Of your career choice, yes, Adam informed me." Sabine leaned closer to Ry. "And yet you've been extremely loyal to your fiancé this whole time, Elena. With so many temptations to choose from..." She flickered her gaze to Elena for a moment before returning to Ry. "I think there's more to this story. Indulge me. How'd you two meet?"

Elena couldn't help the death grip she had on the armrest or the way her heart thrashed so fast that she was sure it was about to pound right out of her throat. She opened her mouth, closed her mouth, not sure what to tell Sabine that would be close enough to the truth to sound plausible.

"We...ah...met—"

"You always tell this story, kitten. Let me." Ry smoothed his hand over hers, hiding her clenched fingers.

Kitten? Elena's mouth dropped open before she could cover it with a forced giggle. No one seemed to notice, though. All eyes were on Ry, including hers.

"As I'm sure you can imagine, El has always been a fan of games." He squeezed her hand, and she wasn't sure if he was doing it to calm her down or to make a point, but either way, she was hanging onto his next words, waiting to hear how he'd spin something that never happened between them. "I was working a security job, keeping watch over a young man who liked to set himself up for risks that he couldn't follow through on without hurting himself or others."

Elena tried to hold her expression so she looked intrigued rather than confused. She knew Ry had been working for extended family, but she hadn't known he'd been assigned to her cousin Jared...who was the exact person that fit that description. The guy loved to prank people and had targeted Elena many times over the years. He was the mini version of her own father, and she'd hated him.

"Elena had planned a masquerade party for friends and family to celebrate her eighteenth birthday."

Elena jolted as memories from that night flooded back to her—the extravagant costumes, the elaborate masks. She'd planned the decorations, the food, and yes, the games as well. It was three years after she'd actually met Ry, so not exactly the truth about their first encounter but definitely more age-appropriate than the truth of her drooling over him at the unripe age of fifteen.

"She had set up the house as a series of escape rooms, and my charge, Elena's cousin, decided that he was going to up the stakes in one of them."

Jared had brought an actual gun to the party. He'd said he wanted to add an element of fear so that everyone would feel like they really had something to escape from. Of course, Elena only found out about his stupid plans once everyone was off in their own rooms and the screaming had started.

"The kid was really stirring up trouble and wrecking the fun, so I planned to take him out of there, but when I found him"—Rylan grinned, which Sabine and Trent both mirrored. He was doing it somehow...spinning a web that Sabine and Trent were falling right into—"Elena had beat me to it."

"You're ruining my party, Jared!" Elena screamed, fists clenched in fury. How dare he threaten her guests?

"Oh, come on, Elena. Chill out. I'm making this game more realistic." He raised the gun like it was a toy, and Elena did what she'd been taught to do. She swooped down low in her cascading taffeta dress, then swept his legs out from under him. At the same time, she wrenched the gun from his fingers. It was a deft move that her trainer had only recently taught her and that she'd practiced religiously.

He hit the ground hard, his head connecting with marble tile. Out cold.

"So, he fucked around and found out," Sabine said with a nod to Elena.

"That he did." Ry chucked again, and this time it sounded real. "She knocked the daylights out of him, and he damn well deserved it."

Sabine and Trent were looking at her with new eyes. They had no idea about her background, her upbringing or that she'd been trained from the time that she could walk to not only defend herself but to disarm an assailant, escape most restraints and generally kick ass.

"I'm impressed, El!" Sabine said. "You know how I feel about pranks, and your cousin sounds like a real jerk."

Obviously, Ry had left out details about the gun and had only told them that Jared was using jump scares to frighten her friends.

All the same, Elena was floored. She'd had no idea Ry had been there that night. The chaos that had unfolded after she'd taken Jared down was a whirlwind, and she'd given one of her father's security thugs the gun while others attended to Jared. She had a party to get back to, so she'd straightened her bodice, poofed up her hair then returned to her friends with a smile.

"I've never seen anything so magnificent as Elena, dressed like a princess in her big skirts and sparkles, take out a kid twice her size." Ry wouldn't look at her, and she so badly wanted him to. "She walked off like nothing had happened, her chin high, shoulders back, hips swaying. I knew from that moment on, I'd do anything for her."

Elena's heart swelled. Her cheeks warmed. She stared at him, and when he finally met her gaze, she saw the usual storm brewing in his eyes. Now it seemed to hold a different meaning.

Was it possible that he was torn over her?

"That's the kind of story I was looking for." Sabine clapped her hands. "I'd say you two deserve some 'special couple' treatment now that you're reunited, don't you, Trent?"

Trent nodded, already on his laptop, hitting keys. "More than a room upgrade, which we've already done."

"Tantric sex session?" Sabine leaned closer to look at Trent's screen.

"Tantric what?" Ry coughed.

"No." Sabine gave Ry a once-over. "I don't think Rylan needs pointers there." She watched Trent scroll before angling her finger at something. "Oh, I know, the adventure tour!" Sabine clapped her hands again. "There's room for two more, right? Since Rylan fell in love with Elena over leg sweeps and you've got some hidden talents, El, you'll both have a blast on this excursion."

"Yeah, very good idea." Trent clicked a few more keys. "Done." He shut his laptop with a grin.

Elena had no idea what the adventure tour was, as she hadn't been part of the game planning for this trip, but she knew by the sound of it that it had to be something that would push Ry way past all of his boundaries.

She gave a wobbly smile.

"Thanks, Sabine!" She felt the tension vibrating off Ry. "It'll be a blast."

Chapter Four

"I don't like this," Rylan mumbled after he'd toured their upgraded suite.

It wasn't so much the room itself, which was a huge space to guard, but more that Elena had beelined for the bathroom calling dibs on the shower and had left the door open enough for him to be tempted to peek.

She'd done this kind of thing before—torturing, teasing, distracting him from his job. She wanted him. She'd only ever been straightforward about her desires.

He'd been anything but.

He wanted her to the point of pain, but he couldn't have her. He'd say it was duty that stopped him from giving in, but it was more than that. He knew nothing good would come from them being together.

She didn't even have to do anything overtly suggestive to get his thoughts rolling in the wrong direction. When they'd entered the resort and stood waiting for directions to their room, they'd both noticed the huge person-sized fireplace in the lounge, a fur rug decorating the floor in front of it.

She'd barely looked at him, just a slight eyebrow lift and curl of one side of her lip had his thoughts turning to the past.

"Have you ever wanted to make love in front of a grand fireplace like this one?" Elena was eighteen, wearing a low-cut shirt and hip hugging shorts and was sprawled on the fur rug in front of her father's office fireplace. "I have... It would be sooo romantic," she said as she rubbed her hands over her stomach as if going straight for her pussy.

Rylan stood with his eyes averted, catching her movements in his peripheral sight, while his skin soaked itself in sweat and his heart thundered. All he could think about was how soft her skin looked, how good it would feel to get naked with her on that fur rug, the fire blazing next to them.

She was a vixen, a temptress—always letting him know that he was the object of her desire and at this very moment, the cause of his extreme discomfort, mainly in his pants.

He'd stayed clear of the open door and its wafting scents of vanilla and strawberry steam that billowed out, coaxing him to come closer, to inhale, to get lost in everything that was Elena. For a solid twenty minutes he'd prayed that she'd hurry up and finish in there.

He had plans for a very cold shower once she was done.

He tried and failed to keep his mind off her water-slicked body, one partially opened door away. He was a man of discipline, self-control. He'd faced many temptations in his life, yet, Elena being so close, under a stream of water, her body all sudsy, her curves glistening, olive skin slick, begging for his hands all over her... Yeah, it was more than he could bear.

All he had to do was push the door open.

She'd grin wickedly, her glorious hills and valleys a feast for his eyes, then she'd beckon him to join her.

Fuuuuuck. His cock was going to punch its way out of his pants if he didn't get his mind on other things.

When he heard the water turn off, he turned his back to the bathroom then did a circuit once again.

You can do this. Man up. Be firm. Focus on protecting her.

Duty.

Obligation.

The room was ideal for their needs, even if it was huge. The windows, while floor-to-ceiling, were tinted so no one could see in but they could see out. They also were equipped with metal storm shutters that Rylan was sorely tempted to use. The only thing holding him back was the attention that would draw. He didn't want to involve Adam and his team in this if he could help it. Too many complications would only make it harder to keep Elena safe. He was satisfied that Cowan security was good at what they did, and it gave him some measure of comfort to know that they'd be on alert for anything suspicious.

Guard dogs to his watch.

Rylan searched the horizon for any hint of boat lights, but all he could see for miles were stars kissing the edge of the ocean. The island itself was not only isolated, an hour boat ride to Nassau, but there was also only one way in that didn't involve navigating through treacherous coral reefs and rip tides. Adam had walked Rylan through the basics on the shuttle that had brought them from the airport to where they were now.

He'd have to explore more over the next day or so to satisfy his paranoia, but he was beginning to lose some of the tension he'd been carrying since Elena had proposed this trip. She might have been right. This place was a good fix for their problem, at least temporarily. His primary goal had been to get her to safety before anyone realized that Cai was dead. Now that he had, his next goal was to convince her that she would have to go into hiding. New York was not a place she could stay safe, not with assassins hunting her...and they *would* be hunting her. Cai had made sure of that when he'd left her his entire fortune. He'd painted a big old target right on her head.

Eventually, she'd have to come to terms with losing her freedom, which, in his opinion, was better than being dead.

"You look deep in thought." Elena's sultry voice encircled him like a finger trailing along his skin. She walked to where he was standing. "Look at that frown." She swung around to block his view of the water, consuming all the air in the room.

Her cheeks were rosy, her lips red, expression cunning. It was too dark in the room to see the details of her eyes, so deeply blue that they often expressed her mood before her face could catch up.

She was glistening, her hair wet, darker than usual, tendrils slicking to her throat. Without makeup, she looked younger, more like the girl he'd known the last time he'd seen her practically naked when she had been nineteen and full of ideas and ultimatums.

He'd slipped back then. He'd caved to his impulses and taken what she'd offered like he'd lost his mind.

He knew her lips to be soft, plush, deliciously addictive. He knew her body to fit into his, her curves and valleys cushions to his hard lines and constant tension.

He'd melted into her, his hands everywhere, hoisting her up so she could wrap her legs around his waist and he could feel the heat of her need pulsing into his gut. He'd devoured her all the while his head was whispering at the wrongness, even if it felt so damn right.

But that was then, and it had been a mistake — one he wouldn't make again. The consequences had been too great for both of them.

She swayed closer.

He tried to look away.

Except...her fluffy robe parted way too low at the front. Her skin was pink from the heat of her shower. She leaned toward him, her head tilted up, her throat exposed, an elegant line that he'd always wanted to track kisses along.

He wasn't breathing. Wouldn't dare draw in the smell of her shampoo, of her.

"Am I spooking you, Ry?" She lifted her fingers to his scar then trailed along his cheek, igniting a path of fire that made him shudder enough to let his breath out all shaky.

Damn her!

He snatched her hand but she twisted away, putting enough distance between them to spare him any further humiliation as he struggled to keep control, to not inhale her intoxicating essence.

Who was he fooling, anyway? Her scent was all over the room. It'd seep into his clothes before the night was through. He'd be tormented by it from now on. It had taken him years to scrub it from his memory before. He was doomed now that his senses were so locked into her.

"You're such a big baby," Elena teased. She perched herself on the end of the bed, her robe gaping enough to show a curve of cleavage. "Scared of someone like me."

"I'm not scared of you," he lied. "I'm scared *for* you."

"Why?" She waved her arm around. "You've spent the last twenty minutes inspecting this room, haven't you? You know just as well as I do that we're safe here."

"It's not that simple." He double-checked the locks on the door before turning to face her again. "We can't let our guard down."

"Oh, Ry." Elena sighed as she stood, her long legs cutting between the folds of her robe. "Look at this place! It's paradise. I plan to enjoy my time here, and you should, too. But first, bed."

"Elena, I—"

Her hand was on the knot binding her robe closed. Her mischievous grin warning him a half second before she tugged it loose then let the robe open.

He turned his back to her but not before seeing smooth, flawless curves, a taut, lean belly trailing to dark curls, a vee of hair and the tease of what he wanted most.

Her knowing laugh made him curse. Never mind the assassins hunting Elena, she would be the death of him.

"See? You *are* afraid of me."

Chapter Five

She had Ry right where she'd always wanted him, and she planned not to waste the opportunity.

"Chill out. I'm under the covers." She loved the feel of high thread count against her skin, and yeah, her hair would be a mess in the morning because she didn't dry it, but she had a mission to get Ry all hot and bothered and couldn't give up the time for a hair blower. "I take it you're planning on staying awake all night."

From the time before, when Ry had been assigned to guard her for months, she knew that with each location change, he'd spend the first night up and on alert before settling into a routine of short naps. How he'd been able to function as he had with such little sleep, Elena could never understand. But he had each and every time. So, she knew his routine and planned to make it count.

She kicked away the comforter, one less barrier, then clicked off the nightstand light, leaving the suite bathed in only moonlight. She watched Ry pace along the windows, then trailed him through the lounge area, to the door. He avoided the bathroom, probably because it still smelled like her, then returned to the couch.

She ran her fingers along the curve of her breasts under the top sheet, sending a ripple down the bed that made Ry pause. Her nipples hardened as she circled them slowly, focusing on him as he resumed his circuit. She had to go slow, to lull him into believing she'd fallen asleep so that his guard was down.

The man was denying the simple pleasures in life. Had always denied himself that. She knew from what little she'd learned of his past that he felt he had things to atone for, that his penance had been a self-imposed denial of all things selfish. She knew he wanted her just as much as she wanted him, but he'd only ever given in once and that kiss had seared her right down to her bones.

He had his back to her, seated, one leg resting along the couch, the other foot firmly planted on the floor. He wouldn't doze off, not tonight. He'd be on alert, listening intently for any sounds that would indicate a problem.

And she knew for a fact that he had very good hearing.

She played with her nipples, flicking the hard buds until they ached, turning her thoughts inward, to what-ifs and what-may-bes. Ry had always been the pinnacle of lust in her eyes — partly because he was so clearly oblivious to how sexy he was and partly because every move he made was so controlled, so calculated. She knew that he would be dedicated to making sure she was satiated if he ever put his hands on her.

She trailed one hand down her belly, imagining the path Ry would take with his lips and his tongue if she ever got him to give in.

He'd use his firm grip to pull her closer, to spread her legs as she was doing now, the sheets rustling as she tented it with her knees. Ry's head turned slightly, zeroing in, no doubt, on the noise. She grinned to herself as she slipped her hand along her slit, dipping her fingers in to feel her hot, wet pussy.

What she wouldn't give for him to kiss her there — for his warm breath to cascade over her slick lips, for him to delve his tongue inside her, for him to rub his fingers over her clit before slipping along her folds.

She used her palm to rock her clit, gently at first, a soft moan slipping past her lips. She cracked her eyes, looking at him through her lashes.

Ry's shoulders hunched. He turned his head to face the windows, obviously forcing himself to focus on something other than her.

She took that as a cue to kick the sheets off.

The air conditioner was blasting cold air right above her, so it washed along her skin, bringing goosebumps to the surface and a tingle along her flesh. She pinched her nipples, alternating from one to the other, while quickening her pace and pressure on her clit, working up a sweat despite the chill.

Her moans grew louder by design — not to the point of being obscene but enough that he knew exactly what she was doing. Her body coiled tight as her orgasm took shape, rising but still out of reach. She could go like this for hours.

Ry adjusted his position on the couch, dropping his other leg to the ground, sitting upright, his arms crossed, eyes glued to the ocean outside. His jaw was clenched, which was such a Ry thing to do — contain, lock down, do everything possible to hold back.

Silly man.

She rocked her hips, rolling up to increase the pressure on her clit. She imagined him inside of her, his fingers buried deep, rubbing her G-spot, reaching up his other hand to cup her breast and sucking hard on her clit with his lips.

She wanted him to worship her, his body pressed close, his weight a delicious pressure, the promise of his cock nudging at her hole. She groaned from deep in her belly, and instead of denying herself, she let her climax peak. It tittered on the edge of release, and even though he wasn't looking at her, she knew his attention was there, in bed with her.

She ground against her palm, pinching her nipple as she arched into her own touch.

"Fuck. Yes. Yes!" Her orgasm crashed with undulating waves that didn't stop—one rolling into the other like an endless loop of ecstasy.

She kept her pace unrelenting, her palm grinding, fucking her own hand as she rode the pleasure through her shuddering, leg-quivering climax.

When she was done, collapsed on the bed, panting and satiated, she idly stroked the curve of her breast and sucked her fingers between her lips, tasting herself and knowing that she had his attention, even without him looking her way. *Is he hard? For sure.* She could see how wide his legs were spread. *Is he aching? No doubt.* Should she go another round and really torture him?

She got her answer a second later when she heard him curse, get up, then beeline for the bathroom. He slammed the door shut. She rolled over to look at the only barrier separating her from Ry and giggled. He wanted her. She wanted him. They were two consenting adults. So what was he afraid of?

Himself, she guessed and the idea of losing control to her.

He could only shut her out for so long.

She was just getting started.

* * * *

Cold shower.

Freezing.

His dick needed a dose of reality.

He'd wanted to wait until she was asleep before he cleaned up, but her sultry game had made it a necessity right now. His cock was weeping for her, his boxers damp from pre-cum. He stripped them off and his dick sprang free, rock-hard and aching.

Damn that woman!

She was going to kill him.

His mind flashed to her naked body, writhing on the bed. He'd only gotten a glimpse, temptation wrenching his head to look at her while she was in the throes of bliss, her orgasm rolling, nipples a darker shade of golden brown than her skin, pebbles that he'd love to suck. Her legs, spread wide, pink and glistening, gave him a glimpse of the soft cushion of her pussy.

The memory was a lightning strike to his cock. He groaned, stifling it at the last minute so it sounded like a cough. Through the door, the flimsy barrier, he could hear Elena giggling. *Fuck! Just...fuck!* He clicked the lock. The last thing he needed was her getting the idea to come in with him—naked, nipples hard, lips parted. *Shit.* He was doomed.

If she stepped through that door, he was a goner for sure.

He turned on the water, blasting freezing temps, stripped his remaining clothes then got in. Pain hit him like a sledgehammer. Each droplet striking his already aching body was a small torture. It would work to refocus him. It had to. Elena on his brain would distract him to the point of error, and he couldn't make any mistakes with her life.

But her body was so lush, so willing. The way she rolled into her palm... Not that he'd been looking...much. But the sounds she made — the moans, the whimpers. God, he'd kill to do things to her that would elicit those sounds again.

He braced his hand against the wall, letting his head drop so the water sluiced over the back of his neck. *Focus on the cold. On the tile.* On anything but *her.*

Instead, he found his hand around his cock, stroking slowly, his head still bowed, imagining Elena on her knees, looking up through wet eyelashes, her mouth partially open, her grin only for him.

Her tits would be slick with water, nipples dripping. He'd reach down to tease her nubs, run his fingers over them, trapping them so he could squeeze. She'd cry out, her mouth opened wide, and he'd nudge her with the head of his cock.

He pinched the tip of his dick, bringing pain to the surface, then switched the water to hot and let pleasure take over.

Fuck it.

The contrast of cold to hot made him shiver, his blood warming suddenly, heat rising to his face, his chest. He stroked his dick like he wanted Elena to, gliding with enough pressure to make him moan again. He lifted his other hand to flick his own nipples the way he wanted to do with Elena's.

Her moans had unhinged him. What he wouldn't give to make her sound like that right here, right now. He'd lick her from asshole to clit. He'd suck her tits until they ached. He'd make her scream his name as she swore through a string of orgasms. He'd fuck her until he couldn't do it anymore. He'd get her out of his system.

No. That would never happen.

His groan echoed off the walls, and he knew Elena would hear him, but he couldn't stop, not when his climax was rising so swiftly that his legs shook. He wanted her like an addict. He'd only ever kissed her once, but that had been enough.

He knew he could walk right out of this shower and take her. He could slide over top of her, spread her legs and punish her pussy. He could claim her lips, devour her as he'd once done before, take her breath away.

He could do it. Lay claim. Take what she was offering. Make her his.

His climax exploded, jets of cum spraying the walls in an unending stream. His cock pulsed to the beat of his thoughts. *I want her. I want her. I want her.* He kept pumping until he couldn't take another stroke then collapsed against the wall…spent, exhausted, defeated.

She'd won this round.

He'd left his new clothes in the living room, so he exited the bathroom with a towel wrapped tightly around his waist. Elena seemed to be asleep, curled up on her side, her hair fanned out on her pillow, the sheet barely covering her curves.

Tearing his eyes away from her, he walked silently toward the bags of clothes he'd bought in Nassau.

The rustle of sheets made him freeze.

"What a waste," Elena's sleepy voice said in the darkness. "You could have filled me up with all that cum."

It took everything in his power to swallow his answering groan.

Chapter Six

Breakfast was in the company of everyone, a large buffet stacked to the tits with mouth-watering food. Elena was starving and loaded her plate with a little bit of everything. She was on vacation! Calories didn't count.

Ry was sulking, or at least his version of sulking. He was seated at the far end of the patio, nursing a coffee — black for his dark mood — refusing to make eye contact with her. She'd gotten him good the night before, but he'd gotten her right back. Point for Ry. The sound of his stifled groan when he came in the shower had rocked through her as she lay listening, her fingers on her clit, vigorously rubbing herself into another orgasm.

This man and his not-in-your-face sex appeal would kill her. If he denied her forever, she might explode. All the same, she was enjoying herself. Despite his brooding and overprotectiveness, she was having fun — at his expense mostly, but still, enjoyable.

Eye still on the prize, though…she had a promotion to negotiate.

"Hey, El," Sonia said as she sidled up next to Elena at the buffet. She was on the trip with her toy-friend, James, and the charmer was currently loading up two plates on the other side of the buffet. "Any idea what the couple's adventure tour entails?"

Elena would normally be the person to ask, since she tended to plan all the party games at Kitty Cat events. "Nah, no idea. I had nothing to do with this one."

"Oh?" Sonia pointed to something she wanted from the table and her boyfriend somehow managed to hold two plates in one hand then scoop more food onto her mountainous pile. "Sabine said it was inspired by a conversation she had with you."

Elena's interest piqued even more. "Really?"

If she'd inspired a game here, that meant that Sabine really did listen to her when she babbled at their monthly team meetings. Problem was, she couldn't remember what specific idea, of her millions, that would have resulted in an adventure tour. She certainly wouldn't have been thinking tropical island in her schemes. Like most of her ideas, though, location wasn't as important as execution.

"Yep, she said you're the genius" — she air-quoted — "who came up with it, so I figured you'd know. James is nervous." She rolled her eyes toward her boyfriend, who shrugged in return. "Thinks it's going to be something embarrassing and kinky."

She and Sonia had an ongoing, friendly rivalry where work was concerned. Sonia never hesitated to take jabs at Elena when the opportunity arose, but she never meant it to be mean. They both knew Elena had more home runs where ideas were concerned. Sonia's talents were more in her ability to gather intel and work the clients. As a team, she and Sonia were unbeatable. Too bad a promotion couldn't include a partnership.

"Oh, I would bet on kinky." Elena laughed. "If it's one of my ideas, that is." She winked at Sonia. "Not embarrassing for any of the Cats, though."

Sonia laughed. Her boyfriend groaned.

Elena headed to where Ry sat, unable to hold her excitement. Her heart was bursting with pride. Sabine had given her credit for one of her ideas...to another Cat no less!

"Ry, I just found out that Sabine is using one of my ideas for the adventure tour!" When he turned a confused look her way, she added, "It's a big deal for me! The whole point of this trip is so I can ask Sabine for a promotion, and if she's using one of my game ideas, that will be a great leveraging point."

"The adventure tour she signed us up for?" He shifted in his seat, his frown back in place. "I was going to suggest we skip it."

Elena's mouth dropped open. "Oh no you don't!" She set her plate down then jutted a hip, her hand resting there. "You aren't going to poo-poo all over my plans."

"Elena, the danger—"

"Stop with the danger excuse." She leaned over, giving him a glimpse of her cleavage, which she'd taken special care to hoist up in her halter for his viewing pleasure. "We both know you're a scaredy cat when it comes to spending time alone with me. The adventure tour will be a distraction for you." She loomed over him, watching as his eyes took her all in, his lids hooding, jaw clenching. "We're doing this. It's a pivotal accomplishment for me, for my career and my future, so shut up with your excuses. I'm getting this promotion, and you're playing along."

Something flashed on his face that unsettled her. A darkness to his eyes that she knew to be pity. She took a step back — her assertiveness, her excitement, sliding to her toes.

That look was deadly. He'd given it to her right before he broke the news that her stepmother had been killed — murdered, while she'd been playing sultry temptress in an attempt to entice him when he should have been on alert and protecting her father's wife.

"El—"

She raised her hand and tried to compose herself. "You're not going to let me continue my career, are you?" Desperate to keep her volume low, she pointed a finger at him, poking the air in front of his face. "That's what your expression just told me. What future career? That's what you're thinking, isn't it?" She cursed under her breath, walked a few feet, her sandals clacking, then spun on her heels and walked back. "You damn bastard. You're still planning on taking me away, aren't you?"

"I'm sorry if you assumed I wouldn't be." He opened his palms as if to say it was out of his hands. "The danger might be on hold right now, but it's not gone forever — not until I take care of it...*if* I can take care of it. I need you safely hidden before I finish things."

"And how long will that take?" But she already knew the answer. It was the same one he'd given her when they were riding out another one of her father's missteps. "As long as it takes," she said at the same time he did.

The last time he'd hidden her, she'd rebelled with dire consequences. They both knew she wouldn't do the same thing this time, not if it meant putting his life at risk again. And she had. Not only did her actions indirectly lead to the death of her stepmother but Ry was hurt and could have been killed.

She glanced at the scar marring his face. She'd done that with her irresponsible actions.

Maybe it was better if she pushed him away instead of fighting to keep him close.

Her heart splintered at that thought. *No.* There had to be a way to make it all work out.

"Ry…" She'd have to convince him that she'd be safe with all the protections Adam and his team provided her back home—the GPS, the option of round-the-clock security. It's not like she'd be alone. They'd just have to tell Sabine and Adam everything so they could protect her…and they would. Sabine and Adam always put the safety of Cowan employees above all else.

And maybe, *maybe* she could convince Ry to stay with her, too.

"Ry…I want—"

"I know what you want, Elena, and it's not possible." His no-nonsense tone had a finality to it that brushed her the wrong way.

"Hey, you two!" Sabine swooped in and draped her arm around Elena's shoulders. "It looks like things are a bit tumultuous over here. Lover's spat? You're far too serious for a vacation." She squeezed Elena's shoulders. "Come join us at the big table around the corner. We've got a game starting—one I think you'll both like."

Elena plastered on a fake smile for Sabine, one she knew her boss would see right through. "Ry is being a party-pooper this morning." She scooped up her plate, despite having lost her appetite. "Better to leave him to sulk."

"You know how it is, Sabine, reacquainting after time apart. Just a difference of opinion." Ry shifted his seat back. "And don't be silly, kitten," Ry said, his voice dripping honey. "I'm up for a game." He stood then took Elena's plate from her hands. "Lead the way."

She couldn't read the look he gave her, but she knew he wasn't impressed with any attempt to separate from him, which gave her an idea. He'd do what he needed to do to stick with her.

"I don't think you're going to like this," she sang, her tone oozing saccharine.

Sabine fluttered off toward the table and out of earshot.

"I don't really have a choice, now do I?" He was making a point in his usual direct way. "And neither do you."

He'd endure what she forced him to, and she would endure what he forced her to.

Even if it made him uncomfortable.

Even if it crushed her dreams.

He was playing along, expecting her to do the same when the time came to disappear. He thought she'd let him haul her off to the middle of nowhere then leave her there to die of boredom and stagnation. He was underestimating her drive, which was silly, because as much as she was loath to admit it, she was the daughter of Cai Russio, and if she got anything from her father, it was unfailing ambition.

They rounded the corner to find a large table set up with seats left for her and Ry and two others. Sabine was heading toward the head of the table while Trent took the seat opposite.

Great, we're the last to join. That was *so* not the way she did things. A few of the other Cats raised some eyebrows her way, noting her late arrival as unusual. She nodded toward Ry, shrugged then grinned. The Cats grinned back.

"Welcome to truth or dare, Kitty Cat style," Sabine said with a sweep of her hands. "Let's go a round of intros before we get started. All the Cats know each other but partners need to tell us about themselves — name, occupation, witty thought?"

As each person introduced themselves, Elena put her hand on the back of her chair, ready to pull it out. Ry swatted her hand away then yanked the seat out for her. He rolled his wrist, making a big deal about offering her the chair.

"Princess," he drawled. She rolled her eyes then sat down. He pushed her in a little too close to the table, trapping her enough to make his point…again.

Her family history made it impossible to escape danger forever, not without his help. Problem was, Ry never liked to ask anyone *else* for help. He was a one-man show when it came to protection. She'd have to figure out a way to change that or she was going to lose everything she'd been working toward.

And she sure as shit would not pay for the sins of her father by giving up her dreams.

"Rylan Ward," Ry said, shaking her out of her thoughts. "I'm in security, and I don't know about witty statements but I'm ready for anything Elena throws my way."

Elena arched her eyebrow for the crowd, smiling as she waved her hand toward Ry. "Silly man…he has no idea." She laughed along with the other Cats. "My name is Elena Sasser and I'm the queen of games at Cowan Enterprises."

"I'd like to point out that Elena is our reigning champion of this game, so you're up against the best of the Cats." Sabine clapped her hands. "Are we ready to get started?"

"You'd better not make me lose, Ry," Elena whisper-growled in his direction. "I *don't* lose."

Ry's silence ratcheted up her anxiety. Would he blow this for her if things got too risky or play along to prove a point?

She could already hear his internal mind grumbles about not being okay with exposing himself to truths or dares. He'd surely see danger in a fun game like this because the man was a perpetual buzzkill.

"That's right, people, I am the champ and I'll do anything to win." She leaned over the table, making eye contact with her grinning colleagues and their shell-shocked partners. "*Anything.*"

"And she's all mine." Ry grabbed her arm then yanked her toward his seat, so she was leaning into him, slightly off balance. He moved close, nuzzling into her hair as if he was giving her a kiss for good luck or something. "Don't do anything reckless," he whispered, his breath warm against her ear, "or I'll have to punish you."

She jolted, electricity zapping every erogenous zone. She tilted her head until she made eye contact.

Did he just…make a threat? A kinky threat?

His expression gave nothing away.

She pulled back a little.

Knowing him, probably not, but the anticipation of *maybe* made her want to be a very bad girl.

She grinned. "Challenge accepted."

Chapter Seven

He'd thrown down the gauntlet on purpose. If he was going to ruin her dreams, at least he could play along while they were — he grudgingly admitted — safe on the island. He wasn't planning on crossing any lines with Elena, no matter how hard she made it to look the other way. He still had his principles, but he could let her have her vacation.

"The dares will be daring and the truths, revealing." Sabine stood at the head of the table, her smile infectious, eyes mischievous and, like on the plane, Rylan was struck by her presence. She was commanding without being threatening, and he could see why Elena valued her opinion as much as she so obviously did. Sabine held power and sway in her voice, projecting enough so she held all ears and eyes.

He'd known a lot of blowhard men, leaders who thought that might equaled right, who couldn't command a group's attention like Sabine was doing right now.

He surveyed the table and noted that out of the twenty couples who'd been on the plane, there were only six couples at the table, including Trent and Sabine. He wondered if the other travelers had decided to opt out in favor of different activities or if they weren't part of the chosen crowd, for some reason.

"You'll draw from the panty pouch." Sabine held up a silky bag that had been fashioned out of women's underwear. "And whatever you get, you're stuck with...unless someone wants to swap with you." She winked. "The dares and truths are on the flip side of each coin." She pulled out a pink medallion shaped like a cat head.

"Each couple will earn points as a team. Complete the dare or truth successfully and you get a point. Fail and you lose a point." She swept the group, grin widening. "The prize is an hour one-on-one with me, and I know that's a hot commodity for all of you Cats specifically."

So that's why they'd been chosen. These were the ones who wanted to talk privately with their boss, presumably, like Elena, looking for a promotion or something equally as valuable.

Elena gave Rylan a meaningful look. She wanted to win, he knew that, but now the stakes were the exact ones she had to have.

"Another thing." Sabine paused, flashing a pointed look at Elena. "If you go above and beyond, I'll reward bonus points!" She clapped her hands. "Be daring. Be creative. Impress me."

The Kitty Cats all cheered, slipping in some sassy hoots and whistles, teasing one another with friendly taunts and overall amping up the energy by a thousand around the table. The partners, on the other hand, all looked on seemingly in the same state of shock as Rylan did.

What have I gotten myself into?

The game began with a woman named Ivana pulling a dare.

"I've been dared to make my partner moan." Ivana grinned. "Piece of cake!" Her partner looked stricken, and Rylan felt sorry for the guy as well as even more anxious for his own situation. What kind of dare would he or Elena pull? He feared this game was going to blur some lines he preferred to be solid and clear.

Ivana stood behind her man, her long-nailed fingers nestled into his hair as she stroked along his scalp. He closed his eyes and let his head fall back. His mouth went slack, and when she leaned in and whispered in his ear, his moan was low, deep and genuine. It took less than two minutes. Poor guy lost his load prematurely in front of everyone. Rylan was horrified that Ivana was able to elicit that kind of response so easily. He was also impressed and a little intimidated, thinking about all the ways Elena could make him moan like that.

All the ways he wanted her to.

Ivana jumped up, clapping her hands and cheering. "Point for us!" Her partner looked dazed, confused and ready to crawl under the table.

"Very good, Ivana," Sabine said, clapping too. "A point for you!"

The bag moved to the next couple, who pulled truth. "I will be sharing the most embarrassing sexual moment of my life. No worries, hon. It wasn't a time with you."

So, it continued, more dares, more truths. If he'd been a blushing man, he'd be red as a tomato with all the TMI and over-the-top displays of affection and lust. At one point, Rylan felt like he was slipping into a weird kind of voyeur role, his attention riveted to the different ways the Kitty Cats got their points. It wasn't always the partner who took the brunt of the asks, but there was a lot of sharing that Rylan found highly intrusive.

The Cats all found it hysterical and not at all inappropriate.

It made him wonder what kind of world Elena had been working in for the last three years. He'd known all about Cowan Enterprises when she'd proposed it as the perfect new life three years before. He'd vetted the company thoroughly. He hadn't been thrilled about some of the job descriptions, but Elena was a grown woman. She could decide what she was comfortable with or not. It wasn't the sex stuff that had him bothered, though. It was the espionage slant that made him uneasy. It had taken a lot of work, but he'd discovered that Sabine wasn't only a sex industry queen. She was also, and probably more importantly, an information collector. He'd gained a surface-level understanding of what the Cats really did in their meetings with powerful men, and his worry was how deep the expectation for spying actually went.

He hadn't wanted Elena to be leaving one dangerous situation only to find herself in another. But, as he found out, security always put the Cats' wellbeing above anything else, and Elena had been committed to going, with or without her father's blessing.

A server refilled Rylan's coffee, pulling him from his thoughts right at the moment that the dreaded bag came to Elena. With dramatic flair, she pulled a coin.

"Truth," Elena said, one eyebrow cocked, lips curled into a sly smile. "Tell us about your first kiss."

Rylan's chest got tight. He adjusted himself in his seat. What was this feeling? Jealousy? He picked up his coffee then put it down. His body was already zinging like he'd had too much caffeine. He was fidgeting...uncomfortable. He didn't want to hear about Elena's first kiss because he knew it was with someone else.

Seriously?

He gave himself a mental slap.

She's not yours, bud. Never will be.

"Well, my first kiss was nothing to get excited about." Elena laughed as she leaned into the table. "It was a boy who came to my house to tend to the stables." She ducked her head a little. "My father loved horses."

So did Elena, Rylan knew. It was the one thing father and daughter enjoyed together without bickering.

"I was all giddy in love with this stable boy who had dark shaggy hair and blue eyes. I thought he looked like Lou Graffilo...you know the star of *Heartless*?"

A chitter went down the table as all the women seemed to recognize the name. Rylan had no clue, but he did remember the kid that Cai had hired to tend to the horses. Scrawny and sly, that one had gotten himself all tied up as Cai's errand boy later on when the horse thing hadn't worked out. Then he'd disappeared completely a few years later.

"I used to make excuses to go see him in the stables." Elena patted her cheeks as if she was embarrassed. No one was falling for it. "He was so dreamy." Elena rolled her eyes and laughed.

Rylan wondered if her father knew about her crush. If he had, Rylan was sure he'd ruin it for her with one of his inappropriate comments, for sure. The man had no filter. It made Rylan wonder if that's why the horse thing hadn't worked out for the kid. Maybe Cai had known about his daughter's interest and had intervened before anything more serious could develop.

"One day I was coming around the corner and bumped right into him." She covered her mouth as she continued to laugh. "And his hands landed right on my tits." She mimicked the action, gripping her own breasts and transfixing Rylan in the process.

The night before, as he was listening to Elena pleasure herself, all he could think about was how her hands were all over her body, playing with her nipples, rubbing herself. He wanted to be the one touching her, kissing her, licking her from asshole to clit.

"We were both stunned, but I took it as a sign that we were having a moment and I leaned in, my lips puckered." She shifted closer to the table, pursing her lips, hands still on her breasts. "And he moved closer. Our lips kind of smashed together, and all I could smell was horse shit." She let her hands fall as she snorted. "He was all slobber and heavy breathing — clumsy and not at all what I imagined my first kiss would be like."

The table rumbled as some of the Cats banged their hands, laughing along with her.

"For bonus points, I'll tell you about my most toe-curling, stop-your-breath kiss. The kiss that ruined me for all other kisses. Or better yet, I'll show you." In a move Ry couldn't fathom being possible, Elena swung her legs and somehow landed on his lap, her arms around his neck, knees straddling the chair. "Gimme a kiss, Ry, just like the one I stole from you all those years ago."

Chapter Eight

He was rigid, his spine straight, fingers clenched to the armrests of his chair, legs tense, and Elena knew she had one shot to melt him before he blew their story and did something to push her away. With her heart in her throat, she did what she'd wanted to do for the last three years.

She let her weight drop into his lap then wiggled her ass against his crotch, which, she noted, also seemed to hold a lot of rigidity, then crushed her lips to his, probing for entry and hoping to the chocolate gods that he didn't reject her.

His lips were as firm as she remembered, as unyielding as she'd fantasized about but, just like in her dreams, the sweep of her tongue against the seam of his lips was too much temptation for him to deny. He let her in and, more encouragingly, slipped one arm around her waist, curling his hand just under her breast while the other snaked into her hair to tug, urgently. She had to tilt her head giving him more access and, apparently, a deeper thrust. He moaned against her mouth and just like that, she knew she'd won.

This round at least.

Just like their first kiss, Rylan quickly took over, guiding their connection as he teased her mouth, probing, pummeling, bruising her lips so it felt like both a punishment and a reward. She rolled her hips, digging into his lap so he would feel the promise she was making.

At some point, on this trip, she would have him.

The buzz of *ohhs* and *ahhs*, the sound of clapping… All of it was a din against the thudding of her heart in her ears and the zing of every nerve pinging in her body. She'd wanted this, a repeat of their first kiss, for so long she almost couldn't bear to let it end. But when he slowed his savoring and pulled his lips away, she let him go, knowing that she'd catch him again and, next time, they'd do much more than kiss.

"Elena," he gruffly mumbled as he briefly pressed his forehead to hers, panting at the same pace as she was.

"That was hot!" Sabine gave a long whistle. "Definitely worth a few extra points."

Elena couldn't help but grin. She'd win this game if Ry continued to play along and, more importantly, she'd win him over if he kept giving in to her ploys. As she started to turn, ready to get up from his lap, she caught a flash across his eyes, his expression showing where his thoughts were, and it made her heart sink just a little.

"Elena." His tone was different, filled with regret but too low for anyone else to hear.

She turned her back, ignoring his buzz-killing ways, then jumped up from his lap. Pushing away his pity and regret would be her biggest challenge on this trip. He thought he was going to crush her dreams. She had other plans.

"It's Ry's turn next!" Elena said, her voice catching on the unexpected lump in her throat. Damn him! She would not give in to his plans. She would not let him ruin what could happen between them—what was *meant* to happen. "Let's hope for something spicy."

She handed the bag to him without looking at his face, not wanting to see any truths shining there. His fingers brushed hers and rather than a shock of connection, she felt the static of loneliness. She knew his truth. He was appeasing her right now...nothing more. Even though they both knew he wanted her, this was only to make her happy in this moment. His heart wasn't in it because, like always, he would forever deny what they could have together.

His job was to protect her, and right now, that meant going along with her game.

He dug his hand into the satin bag, moving the coins around so they clinked, probably hoping for something easy like a truth he could lie about. Elena plunked herself into her chair. Rather than continue to feel sorry for herself, she devised a new plan. If he was going to lie to himself, pretending that he wasn't truly falling for her charms, then she was going to give him a taste of his own medicine.

Rylan hated this game. He hated that Elena had put him in a position to lie to her. The kiss was amazing, glorious, the best he'd ever had, and it was all for show because she'd forced it to happen. She'd put him in a position where it was either go along or embarrass her. And, sure, he'd put on a good show for the crowd, but what did she expect? With her plump ass digging into his dick, driving him insane? And her plush lips devouring him? She made him want things he couldn't have, and now she'd forced him into a public display of affection that he couldn't follow up on. Lies like that would crush her if she kept pushing them to happen, and he hated that she needed him to be this person for her right now. He didn't want to hurt her, but that was what was going to happen in the end.

What he hated most of all was that his body didn't know the difference between duty and pleasure. Yeah, he wanted her. Fine, he'd admit that. And yes, he craved touching her, kissing her, doing things to her that were so out of bounds he wanted to punch himself in the throat. She wasn't making it easy, either—not that he'd expect her to. But to look at him like he'd stabbed her in the heart when all he was doing was trying to make her happy on this trip? Well, that was more than he wanted to deal with.

He pulled a chip out, read the inscription.

Dare. *Fuck.*

Elena plucked it out of his hand then read it to the group. "Dare... Skinny dip with an audience."

A titter went through the crowd. Rylan lowered his head. Not that he was shy about his body... It was a body, anatomy, and he wasn't ashamed of his scars. But his raging boner was going to send all kinds of wrong messages to Elena.

She looked at him, one eyebrow cocked. "If he strips right here and makes a run for the water, will he get extra points?

"Hell yes!" Sabine said, followed by a round of clapping and cheering.

"Extra points, Ry. You know what you have to do."

By the sly smirk, he knew what she was up to.
Payback.

It was petty, childish but he understood. She thought she'd be able to change his mind, to win him over. She thought she'd be able to convince him that her way would work. She'd probably crafted some plan that included him living in New York with her, protecting her from danger while she continued to work her dream job. But that wasn't possible no matter how much his body yearned for it. He had an endgame that would ensure Elena would be safe, but only if she remained anonymous, living a quiet life, a simple life and it didn't include him.

It hadn't been his idea to come here, and he certainly wasn't going to feel bad about doing what he needed to do to protect her, even from himself and his urges.

He decided this morning that he'd play along. He'd committed to giving her one last joyride before he took her freedom.

If she wanted extra points, he'd give them to her.

With a shrug, Rylan stood. He flashed Elena a tooth-baring grin, which he suspected looked downright predatory, then slowly began to unbutton his shirt.

Her eyes were riveted, sparkling, stripping him bare before he could do it himself.

Heat seared over his skin, like her eyes were supercharged, branding him.

He had a sudden impulse to impress Elena. He didn't care about anyone else watching him. It was Elena's eyes on him that had him transfixed. Her lips parted as he tugged his shirt off his shoulders then down his arms. She dabbed the tip of her tongue to the side of her mouth then bit her bottom lip.

He might know her plans. He might understand her game. But he definitely wasn't immune to her charms. This trip was going to test all his self-control. Despite that, he couldn't stop himself from giving her what she wanted right here, right now.

His control was slipping, and, in this moment, he didn't care.

He tossed his shirt at her face and the crowd clapped. Someone turned on music, a steady thumping bass. Wolf calls and hoots went down the table. Rylan winked at Elena as he unbuttoned his pants.

She leaned forward, roving her eyes down his chest. It made his cock throb harder, her eyes on him like that.

If she wanted to see the reality of her game and what it did to him, he'd give it to her, and she'd have to settle for looking but not touching. He dropped his pants and her gaze landed on his dick. It pulsed along with her breath, which came out like a gust.

He wanted her lips cushioned around his cock. He wanted her scorching heat of her gaze to take him all in. This is what she did to his body.

But he wouldn't give in.

He turned his back to her, showing her his ass, then saluted the table before trotting down the patio, jumping from the deck to the soft, scalding sand then sprinting to the clear blue water.

He'd almost reached the sanctity of the waves when he heard a yip and a laugh and Elena breezed by him, buck naked, her ass rippling, tits jiggling. She grinned over her shoulder at him before diving into the water.

Chapter Nine

He'd barely survived the skinny-dipping challenge. Not because he couldn't swim but more like there'd been a shark in the water—and her name was Elena.

She'd tormented him with a backstroke that highlighted her glistening tits and neatly trimmed pussy. Then she'd flipped over, stuck her ass in the air and dove under each wave that had come their way.

It'd been glorious to watch. His cock had throbbed endlessly, so much so that he'd cut his swim short to beeline for their room so he could rub one out before she made it back. Didn't matter though, she knew.

She knew, and she loved it.

And that's when he realized that she might have an advantage over him with this game they were playing. She knew he was fighting his urges for her. She knew, and she didn't care—not about danger or about his duty. None of that mattered to her. She had nothing to lose but her freedom, and he knew she'd fight dirty to keep that.

Of course, she'd won the competition. She'd come back to the room draped in a robe, her clothes flung over her arm and holding a trophy.

Then, unexpectedly, she thanked him. "I appreciate you playing along. This trip isn't all fun and games. It's important to me, and I'm grateful that you understand that."

Understand, yes. He definitely understood her drive toward her dreams. She came by her ambition honestly. It was in her DNA. Both her father and her stepmother were very goal-driven people. Where they'd used their skills for evil, Elena was using hers for anything but. He knew she gave her money and her time to charity. He'd kept tabs on her from a distance over the last three years. He suspected that while this promotion would be a boost for her self-esteem, she was really doing it so she could earn more money to help others as she had been all this time.

"You're welcome," he said when he realized she was standing there waiting for a response.

She nodded, her expression a little sad, then walked into the bathroom, shutting the door silently behind her. And for the first time since they'd reunited, he felt like she was the one rejecting him, closing him out...rather than the other way around.

If she was finally accepting what needed to happen, then that suited his plan, but he couldn't help the painful thud in his chest at the loss of her effervescence.

Dinner plans were a Kitty Mingle, whatever that was. Elena had been quiet all afternoon, reading on the balcony for hours before coming inside to get ready.

She hadn't spoken to him since she'd returned from the beach, and Rylan was beginning to think something was very wrong—that was until she stepped out of her dressing room in an outfit that barely contained her curves. The dress looked like it had been painted on. The top part was emerald green, sparkling in an iridescent way as she moved into the light. One shoulder was covered, the other bare. The neckline plunged between her breasts to her bellybutton and somehow stayed put as she bent to slip on her heels. One hip was exposed while the other was hugged by a swath of black that only went mid-thigh.

Rylan soaked her in, adjusted his tie and stifled a cough before turning his gaze away and praying that he didn't lose his shit completely and rip what little of her clothes there were from her body. Hot didn't even cover how she looked. She was on fire and threatening to burn the place down.

She was on him in a second, a predator scenting prey. With her heels, she came to his chin yet still managed to dominate his space. Her strawberry scent walloped his nose as she straightened his collar, smoothing down the front of his suit with flat palms and a firm pat.

"I like it when you get all dressed up," she said, her lips glistening with gloss, her breath minty and warm. "You used to always wear these suits, remember?"

His fingers itched to touch the silky skin of her shoulder. To trail along her exposed collarbone and raise goosebumps.

"I fantasized about you coming into my room at night. Checking in on me, making sure I was safe and finding me splayed out in my lingerie, my thong up my ass, tits nearly spilling from my camisole." She pressed her body against his. "I waited and waited for you, Ry." She tilted her head up. "But you never got the hint."

"I wouldn't have taken advantage," Rylan managed to grumble, even though his heart was in his throat and his cock straining against his pants.

"It's not taking advantage if it's what I want." Then she stepped away, leaving a void that Rylan didn't want to confront. "Time to go schmooze."

She was out of the door with him scrambling after her, his head spinning and his body check engine lights blinking uncontrollably.

The other Kitty Cats were dressed just as provocatively, but none of them were as eye-catching as Elena. She was the center of every conversation, moving from one cluster of people to the other, captivating them with her beaming smile and infectious, husky laugh.

She'd left him in the dust, making it clear with a pointed glare that he wasn't to follow her.

So, the game continues.

He opted for a seat at the bar, nursing a watered-down gin and tonic, watching her like a hawk.

"She's amazing, right?" Trent took the stool next to him then ordered a whiskey. "Sabine really values her opinion. She's got a gut instinct for working a crowd."

"I'm seeing that." Unexpected pride bloomed in Rylan's chest. "I didn't know she could do that..." He waved his drink in her direction as she moved from one group to the next. "Work a room like that." Had her father known, he would have bled that particular talent dry. Cai was brutal and commanding, but he was never charismatic. Elena had really bloomed in her new life. Rylan couldn't help the smile tugging his lips out of a perpetual frown.

"She's genuine. That's why she's so successful. And driven, of course, but all the Cats here are." Trent downed his drink then motioned for a refill. "Her creativity is unmatched."

Rylan knew that spark came from her mother, Isabella Russio, Cai's first wife. Elena had only been eight when she'd died from cancer. Elena had told him once that her mother had been devoted to making Elena happy, occupying her time so she never asked questions about her father and his activities. "*My mother insisted on turning everything into a game,*" Elena had told him once. "*She made everything we did full of laughter and light where my father turned everything into darkness and tears.*"

Elena had turned into the embodiment of her mother, carrying on her legacy of making everything fun.

"Sabine must be aware she's after bigger things." Rylan didn't know what compelled him to push Elena's agenda. It just kind of slipped out. She wanted a promotion. He wanted to know if she could get it. It was like he was seeking proof that he shouldn't strip her of a life that brought her so much joy and success, not even to save that very same life. "Do you think she deserves it?"

Trent chuckled into his drink, sipping instead of downing this time. "More than most, yeah. She works hard, but that's not why she's at the top of Sabine's watch list." He paused as Sabine entered the room, his eyes only on her as she made her way toward the group Elena was talking to. "Elena is loyal, almost to a fault. That's what makes her number one."

Loyal. Right. Her relentless devotion to getting him into her bed could be seen as loyalty. He'd just never thought of it that way.

With a nod, Trent left, heading toward Sabine, leaving Rylan to contemplate what little he understood of Elena in this world. While she was still the same girl he knew from the time she was fifteen—headstrong, wily, mischievous—she was also so much more…loyal, committed, driven.

The most dangerous thing about Elena were those hidden layers he was just starting to see, because piquing his curiosity was sure to get them both in trouble. And yet, he couldn't stop himself from following Trent to the small group so he could join the conversation and see her in action.

Chapter Ten

"So, you're the love of El's life, huh?" A bubbly blonde holding a martini zeroed in on Rylan. "She's told us so much about you."

"Rylan Ward." He held out his hand. He wasn't remotely prepared for the love of Elena's life question and had to wonder what the hell Elena had been saying about him.

She waved his hand away before leaning in for a hug.

"We're practically family!" she gushed, her martini splashing over the rim. "I'm Sonia, one of El's best friends."

"Great to meet you, Sonia." Rylan extricated himself as gently as possible. "You met Elena at work then?"

"At work, at play, you know how it goes." Sonia took a sip of her drink before continuing. "Elena has never been one of the escort Cats, so we steal time when we can for after work fun."

Not one of the escort Cats? Rylan frowned. He'd reconciled Elena's choice to join the notorious escort agency a long time ago. It, mostly, didn't rile up the jealousy that he *wasn't* supposed to feel toward her.

"You mean she doesn't go on dates?" He was confused, because as he was keeping tabs on Elena over the years, he'd assumed being one of *those* Cats was mandatory. Now he realized that he never found any evidence to confirm that.

"No, silly." Sonia finished her martini. "She said she never wanted the water to be muddy with her feelings and fidelity to you."

"To me?" Rylan felt that confession like a punch to the gut. Not that he'd been with anyone in the last three years, but he'd worked very hard to accept that Elena had her own life and that it didn't include him. To hear that she'd been saving herself for him — or at least, that's what she'd been telling her friends — well, that was downright shocking.

"Yep. You should be honored. A girl like Elena could make a killing being an escort." Sonia's eyes flickered to where Elena was chatting with another group. "Look at her! She's vivacious. The old guys would eat her up."

Elena was stunning in her skintight dress that moved with her body so fluidly it was a masterpiece of engineering. The sudden thought of her being pawed at by men in Sabine's Gentlemen's Club made him want to growl.

"What did she tell you about me?" He was curious now and felt a little off center. Elena had spent three years telling her friends that he was her fiancé — three years of loyalty that he didn't ask for and didn't know what to do with. He'd be lying, though, if he said he didn't like it. That was the mindfuck of it all. He'd always considered Elena off limits, except they'd crossed the line that one time and he'd had a taste. Like any good addiction, he'd been instantly hooked. He was lying to himself every time he tried to keep Elena at arms' length. What he really wanted, had always wanted, was her.

"Oh, you know, how handsome you are." Sonia gave him a once-over that kind of made him feel dirty. "How fit." A server brought her another martini. "Thank you." She took a taste before plucking out the olive. "She told us about how you always looked out for her, protected her, like that time you beat up those asshole bullies that were giving her a hard time."

"The asshole bullies?" Rylan didn't follow. Bullies? What? While his primary jobs had been away from where Elena had lived with her parents, he'd spent some time at the compound. He hadn't been directly in charge of guarding her...until Rome.

"Yeah, when you were in Italy, on vacation, and those guys were harassing her about her father or something."

Italy during a heat wave. Elena in a baby-blue bikini that did nothing to cover her up and everything to drive him wild. She'd spent most days by the pool in their private resort, soaking up the sun, her body glistening with sweat. She'd known exactly when he'd patrol, when he'd be where she was—in the back, trapped by obligation. She'd applied tanning oil like her skin was starved for it. He'd tried to distract himself in many different ways, checking gates, examining security keypads, but she'd always been there, like a predator stalking prey, making sure he saw her, making sure he knew what she was offering.

"Oh...right...*those* asshole bullies." Rylan coughed through an awkward laugh. Elena had painted an off-center picture of her life before Cowan Enterprises. Those men had been assassins sent to kill Elena and her stepmother. They shouldn't have known where the compound was. Cai's security team had gone to great lengths to locate a secluded resort, and instead of renting the space, he'd bought it outright. Cash. There's been no paper trail. They'd taken a private jet, no flight plan. There should have been no way to trace them.

Rome had been the first time that Rylan had understood how much Cai was hated and to what lengths his enemies would go to destroy his life. At the time, Cai had been untouchable. His family, on the other hand, apparently, were not.

They'd gotten Celeste, but Elena had escaped because she'd snuck into his room, waiting there, on his bed, in lingerie. At the time, it had infuriated him, finding her there, nineteen and full of bad ideas. He'd specifically told her not to leave her suite of rooms at night. The mansion was sprawling, and he'd wanted some control over their movements so he could schedule his patrols without worrying about where Celeste and Elena were. "She didn't deserve what happened. I had to take care of it."

She'd distracted him. Come on to him with the force of a hurricane. They'd shared a kiss — a mind-blowing, forbidden, once in a lifetime, kiss.

All the while, her stepmother was being murdered.

The security guy who'd let Elena slip out of her suite had also missed the assassins coming in through the windows. He'd paid dearly, too. No coming back from decapitation.

Rylan had hunted them down in the days that followed. He'd taken out each of those assassins and gave retribution to Elena's family. It wouldn't bring her stepmother back, but at least he could say that the loose ends were cauterized.

He'd worried that Elena would be traumatized by the whole thing. She'd been prepared her whole life for the danger that being a Russio meant, but that night she'd faced the brunt of her parent's sins. She'd lost her stepmother brutally. While they hadn't been exceptionally close, Rylan knew that Elena didn't hate the woman—not enough to wish her dead, anyway. And worse was that it could have been Elena who had been tortured and murdered. Had she been caught in the hallway...or even in her room, it would have been her.

All the same, he'd always felt that what they'd done, the intimacy they'd shared, was wrong, that he'd taken advantage and had lost control.

The fact that she'd been telling everyone that he'd protected her that night gave him a different perspective.

"Elena said you're always looking out for her. She trusts you—which I know is hard for her, given what her father is like." Sonia continued babbling.

Rylan's mind swirled through the information. Obviously, Elena had painted a picture of her past to hide the truth and help her fit in. She'd constructed a relationship with him to explain his existence in her life, probably because she expected that, one day, he'd come to her on a job to save her life.

She'd been preparing this whole time, carefully constructing a past that everyone would believe.

So maybe all her talk about him was just part of her façade.

He wanted to brush it all off as that, but his gut wasn't having it.

"You should see how she gets when she talks about you... She's all dreamy, droopy eyes, big smile." Sonia laughed. "She's got it so bad for you."

Maybe she *was* neck deep in the same lust for him that he felt for her.

Hope flared where it shouldn't. He didn't deserve Elena's loyalty or her kind words. He didn't deserve her attention at all. He needed to set her straight. This would only end badly for them...for her. He had no delusions about where this would end for him. His life had always been one of violence. Giving in to his feelings for Elena would only put her more at risk than she was now.

More at risk than being hunted for her newly acquired wealth, the legacy of her father's evil deeds? More at risk than being a Russio?

Who was he trying to kid?

Myself.

"What nonsense are you telling him, Sonia?" Elena slipped her hand around her friend's waist and clinked their glasses together. "Don't believe anything she says." Elena's narrowed gaze struck him like an icepick.

"I speak only the truth," Sonia said with a giggle. "But damn, woman, your description of him in a suit...hawt!"

"What description?" Rylan was even more intrigued about the stories she'd been telling.

"Oh, it's nothing," Elena said with a wave of dismissal, her cheeks turning a little rosy. "One of my father's dinner parties—"

"Girl, the way you described it, it was a full-on banquet. Extravagant dresses, important people, dancing...and Ry, dressed in a black suit and tie, watching over everyone."

Cai Russio had a lot of parties just like Sonia was describing, many of which Ry had been in attendance.

"I can't believe your father embarrassed you like that..." Sonia took a gulp from her drink.

Rylan felt his world shift. He knew exactly what party Elena had told Sonia about.

"His fiftieth."

Elena gave a simple nod, her cheeks a stronger shade of cherry.

She'd been stunning in her silver ball gown, all dressed up for the event of the century. Her father had spared no expense for his own fiftieth birthday party. He'd invited a lot of important people, so many that it had been all hands on deck, security-wise.

"I wish that night had gone differently," he said, and he truly did. He'd seen how hurt she'd been when her father rejected her, brushing off the attempt she'd made to have a father daughter dance.

"I learned the waltz for that man. So ungrateful." Elena tried to laugh it off, but Rylan heard the lingering hurt in her voice.

"The waltz is so old-fashioned!" Sonia bumped Elena's hip. "Parents can be so blind to their kid's efforts. Am I right?"

From what Rylan had heard after the fact, Elena had spent months getting the dance just right so she could honor his birthday and show how much she cared about him. He'd rejected her attempt to get him on the dance floor, even when one of his favorite songs was playing, one Elena had explained he had sung to her often when she was little. He'd brushed her off with a crass comment about not wanting to waste precious drinking time and demanding the band play something more upbeat.

Rylan had watched from the sidelines, wanting so badly to save her from the embarrassment her father was heaping on her.

"So, what else did you tell him?" Elena abruptly shifted the conversation. "Sonia loves gossip, so I'm sure she filled your ears with a lot of drama."

Sonia's laugh was like a whip, edged with a little too much force. "Drama *is* my middle name. I was just filling Ry in on how heartsick you've been over him for the last three years." She swatted Rylan on the shoulder. "I mean, buddy, where the hell were you? Your woman was dying…dying for you to come sweep her off her feet."

Elena rolled her eyes and bumped Sonia with her hip, making both of their drinks swirl dangerously in their glasses. When her gaze moved back to his, her eyelashes fluttered, her lips opened slightly and her face held the truth. She'd saved herself for him, and right now, her vulnerability was laid bare. She was waiting for rejection. She was expecting a snide comment. For him to push her away somehow.

But he couldn't. Not because he didn't want to blow her cover story but because, in this moment, he was losing his willpower.

He was struck by her beauty, by the idea that she'd saved herself for him, by the way she smiled suddenly and it lit up her eyes. She knew he was cracking.

Fuck. I'm in deep trouble.

"I'm here now" was all Rylan could say, his voice gravelly, mouth full of rocks. He didn't mean to sound that way but at least he had her attention. They needed to talk. He wanted to get her alone, to find out what other things she'd said about him.

But he also wanted her to himself. He wanted to stroke her skin. He wanted to taste her again. He wanted to take everything she was offering.

Elena stopped giggling. So did Sonia.

"Quick, girl, make a run for it before dinner starts. I'll cover for you." Sonia nudged Elena's shoulder.

Run. Take her. Now.

Without thinking, Rylan took Elena's drink then passed it off to Sonia before swooping Elena up in his arms. He walked away from the party, determination making him steady. Each step was a battle in his mind, though. His logic railed against his body. *Put her down. Stop this now. You're only going to make things worse.* While his heart swelled. *Mine. Always has been. Saved herself. Heartsick over me.*

He kept walking. She slipped her arm around his neck. She pressed her head against his chest. She melted into him.

"I hope you know what you're doing, Ry," she whispered but her voice was full of heat and promise.

He only knew what he wanted to do. He had no idea what would actually happen once he got her alone. He needed to re-establish boundaries. He feared that the snowball effect of his actions now would cascade to the point of no return. He couldn't stop himself from hoping that his mind would lose — that his heart would shut down all the reasons why not.

Her scent. Her heat. Her weight pressed into him was intoxicating. He'd waited. He'd denied himself.

For duty. For obligation. For loyalty.

She kissed his neck, and it was a lightning bolt to his cock.

His desire for her burned him to the core, and the last of his resolve scorched away.

He would taste her. He had to.

Consequences be damned.

Chapter Eleven

Elena had fantasized about Ry doing this very thing so many times over the years that it felt surreal to be in his arms finally. She was floating rather than being carried, her heart pounding so furiously that she was sure he could feel its vibration. Pulses raced over her skin, through her body, straight to her pussy so she shivered with pent-up need.

He walked them all the way to their room — his eyes focused ahead, jaw set in such a way that she would have thought he was walking to his doom.

Maybe to him, he was.

After years of denying her every attempt to persuade him, he was finally giving in to his lust. She nuzzled his neck, knowing by the way he shuddered, how the goosebumps pebbled his skin, that it was his kryptonite. She did it again, her lips quirking against his salty flesh when his arms trembled. *He loves it.*

He set her down at the door but didn't move to open it. He'd taken his hands from her but stood close enough for her to feel his heat. She looked up at him, saw the storm in his eyes then did the only thing she knew would push him over the edge.

She slid her hand from her hips to her breasts, dancing her fingers over her nipples as they puckered, peaking the fabric, then slipped her other hand down his torso, to his groin.

His cock was stiff, long to the point of ridiculousness and as thick as she'd always imagined. She licked her lips, knowing that his imagination would go wild with what she could do to him tonight if he let her. He groaned, taking her all in, his eyes hooded, his breath stuttered.

"Elena…" He wanted her. She heard it in his voice.

She was his ultimate temptation. She stroked his cock through his pants, bending slightly to get to his tip. As she moved back up, she let her breasts rub along his torso, her eyelashes fluttering, lips pouted.

"It's only ever been you, Ry." She tilted her head up then dabbed her tongue to the corner of her lips before biting down on the bottom one. "I want to know what you taste like." She rubbed her hand down his shaft again. His knees visibly wobbled. "I want to know what it's like to feel you inside me—filling me up, pounding me with this steel rod."

His eyes flashed danger. She was pushing him over the edge. He lifted his hands and for a split second she thought maybe he was going to tell her to stop, that he was going to step away. It was what he would have done in the past well before they'd gotten to this point. Instead, he gripped her hair, tugging her scalp and coaxing her up on her tiptoes. She moved with him, wrapping her arms around his waist, letting a sly smile curl her lips. His other hand fell to her ass with a heavy thud that promised naughty things in the future.

"You kept yourself for me." His voice was thick and heavy. It poured over her like cream, making her body shudder with anticipation. "I told you we had no future. I told you it would never happen again. I told you to move on with your life."

"I didn't listen." She pushed her tits against him as she kissed his throat, his jaw, the corner of his mouth. "You promised me a punishment."

Rylan growled, his chest vibrating, his eyes blasting heat, then he kissed her with a ferocity that knocked her breath out and made her knees buckle. Deep, probing, devouring her so her heart was in her throat and her body didn't know what way was up. He got the door open, and they stumbled into the room, hands everywhere, lips all over, clothes being torn off and tossed haphazardly.

He peeled her dress from her shoulder, stripping the skintight fabric with urgency. The look on his face told her that he'd wanted to do this all night. He was hungry for her skin, to see what the dress was barely covering.

Goosebumps cascaded over her, sending a shiver from her scalp to her toes.

She'd already coaxed his shirt off, his belt, her fingers working at his zipper, fumbling in her speed. He smacked her hands away then shoved her back as he tore her dress down her body in one sweep, exposing her to his hot stare.

He took her in, his fingers hovering close but not touching. She saw the torment in his eyes. He debated his actions. Guilt, obligation, rode his conscience hard, she knew that, but the lust burning there was enough to tell her to push him just a tiny bit more.

He wanted this…always had.

She shimmied the dress down her legs, moving backward toward the bed as she kicked it off and stood naked for him to see what he'd been missing in all his years of denial.

"Take me," she said as she ran her hands down her sides and over her hips. "I'm yours."

He rubbed his jaw, looked up to the ceiling as if he'd find escape there. When he looked back at her, his face was set with predatory resolution. He stalked to her, his fists clenched along with his jaw. She had the urge to bolt — to run so he would chase her — but instead she stayed put, reveling in the shiver, a warning that rolled down her spine.

He took her in his arms, his bare chest hot against her tits, the coarse curls teasing her nipples. He tilted her off balance, her face close to his, hands splayed against her ass. "You've tormented me."

"With pleasure," she whispered.

"Teased me." His voice was a rumble, dangerous sounding and so damn delicious.

"Calculated every move."

"Tortured —"

"I'd do it all again and again to get you here." She arched against him. "I'm yours, Ry."

He glared, swore and, in one swift move, flipped her over then pushed her face-first into the bed. She grunted, off balance and in shock, then managed to lift herself onto her elbows just as the first slap came. Hard, fast and unexpected, his palm seared her flesh, sending a jolt through her body and knocking her forward. She shook the first hit off, her ass on fire, then lifted herself again, offering herself up.

"You want to be punished?" He swatted her again, fast, furious, stinging slaps. "You deserve to be punished?" He didn't break or give her time to adjust, the burn from his palm radiated up her spine.

She moaned, loving it, then pushed her ass up higher, arching her back and welcoming his heavy palm landing on one cheek then the next, tanning her ass so she knew it'd be hard to sit later.

He grunted with each hit, saying things under his breath that she couldn't hear but knew were more about punishing himself than her. He'd always been a sucker for self-torture. She'd barely had to do anything to get him all hot and bothered, a storm raging in his eyes apparently over what he'd like to do versus what he would do.

She expected the spanking to go on until her ass felt like it was twice its normal size, but instead, he yanked her legs by the ankles, taking her down in one swift motion, then rolling her over so her tender skin abraded against the bed's comforter.

"Spread your legs," he ordered. His eyes were wild, his breath feral, chest heaving.

She did as he said, opening her legs to him, feeling more exposed than she ever had before. She'd teased him with her body many times, but she'd never given him this. He stared at her pussy like it was the Holy Grail. She saw the debate in his eyes, how he tortured himself with doubt.

She ran her hands over her breasts, rocking her hips to coax him to give in, give up. "Take me."

He growled again, ran his hand through his hair, walked away only to storm back to her. "You're evil."

"I know."

He dropped to his knees, his hands on her thighs, burning her skin as he wrenched her legs open wider. She watched him devour her with his eyes. He licked his lips. So close to losing control finally.

"I'm yours, Ry." She had him right where she wanted him — between her legs and dying for a taste.

He snapped his gaze to hers, and she read confusion mixed with a possessive need so thick that his eyes were storms of desire.

"Take what's yours."

He groaned. She rolled her hips up. He slid his hands down her thighs, caging her pussy until he pulled her lips apart with his thumbs.

"Ry," she moaned, desperate for more of his touch. "I've waited so long…"

He watched her writhe, her fingers flicking, pulling, cupping her breasts, her nipples so hard they hurt.

Something shifted. A resolution seemingly made. He swore again then brushed her hand from one breast before taking over, splaying his fingers over her nipple, cupping her tit possessively. He leaned his head between her legs, moving slowly as if he was tasting her scent on his tongue like a snake. She watched him watching her and wanted to scream at him to hurry because she was dying…dying for his touch.

He slipped his thumb to her clit, jolting her with pressure — hard, sure, relentless. As he squeezed her tit, he pinched her nipple and darted his tongue to her clit, licking her little bud forcefully. She cried out, arched into his mouth, then died as he closed his lips over her sensitive nub and sucked her so hard that she saw stars.

She'd been waiting for this moment for so long that she couldn't reconcile that it was actually happening. Ry was finally touching her in all the ways she'd dreamed of. He delved thick fingers deep into her pussy, rubbing along her G-spot until she was moaning in one long unending string. Her orgasm was right there, hair-trigger ready to explode, and she couldn't stop it, wouldn't stop it, because Ry needed to know how he affected her. So many long years of fantasizing to get to this moment... She'd come from just the thought of him licking her clit. Now that he was, she couldn't contain her reaction.

He tugged on her nipple, his tongue stroking, fingers rubbing her inside, and it all coalesced into wave upon wave of climax rolling through her with shuddering, bone-jarring speed.

She gasped, her breath caught in her throat, but Rylan kept going, wringing every last shudder, every last moan from her body. She regretted her inability to hang on, to slow it down and savor what he was giving her, but how could she stop the train of her climax when he gave her everything she'd ever wanted? She curled in on herself, pulling away from him as he sat back on his heels. Her body was on fire, every nerve ending zinging. That had been better than she'd ever imagined, and it was only the start. She gave herself a few heartbeats to let her head float back from outer space then dragged her body to the edge of the bed, crawling on all fours, her eyes on Ry, who looked ragged, his shoulders collapsed, knees still on the floor, on the brink of losing control. She would suck his cock so good that he'd lose his mind completely.

She leaned into the edge of the bed, dangerously close to tipping off, then kissed him, certain that she had him exactly where he wanted to be, where she needed him to be.

When he didn't respond, she pulled back, dread pooling in her gut. She saw the war raging in his eyes. Doubt poking him so he was frowning, panic at the edge of bursting through.

"Ry—"

"Don't," he said as he stumbled back, trying to move away from her, to get to his feet.

She jumped from the bed, determined to stop him from running. "Don't freak out." She gripped his arm, nails digging into his skin. "Let it happen, Ry. You know you want me."

He turned on her, his hand snaking into her hair to crane her neck so he could glare at her. "You don't understand, Elena. You never have."

"Help me understand." She let her body relax so he had to hold her. He let her hair go, both hands now scorching her skin, touching her like she was the flame, when really, he was the one burning her.

"You're not mine."

"I'm telling you that I am. I've always been." Back to his buzzkilling ways, disappointment edged along Elena's high.

"I've already done too much. Taken too much. I can't let my lust compromise—"

"Compromise what? My parents are dead. You did what you could. Their own shitty lives caught up with them." She got her feet under her, sighed, then pulled away from him but not out of his touch. "You're all I have left, Ry."

Her words seemed to hit him harder than she intended. She'd never said anything like that out loud but right now, she meant them. He was her steady rock—the one person who knew her, like *really* knew her, the one person she trusted and could rely on.

"I have no future." He set her on her feet then stepped away.

"You could, though. You could have a future with me." She hated how desperate she sounded. She was angry that he kept denying what he so obviously craved.

"I wasn't born for love. I was born for war." He shook his head. "My job is to protect you, and I can't do that if I'm distracted by you."

"I didn't ask you to protect me!" She thumped her chest like she'd seen her father do a million times. "I never wanted you to come back if this was all you were willing to give me."

He flinched, and she regretted her words. Before she could take them back, he lowered his head and sighed. "Your father asked me. His dying wish was to keep you safe" —he looked up at her, his eyes almost black— "even if it meant giving up my life for yours."

"Oh, for fuck's sake!" She threw her arms up. "You and Father have this romanticized idea of what your job is. You weren't born to die for anyone."

"My life isn't as important as yours." It was clear that he believed his own bullshit. "I'm not worth anything without my vow to your father."

"What a load of crap. You're a paid thug, Ry, always have been. My father didn't respect you. He didn't value your life. You were always an employee to him, and now he's got you vowing your life to save mine? Why would you do that? It's not worth a sacrifice."

"Don't…"

She knew she was pissing him off, but she wanted emotion out of him, a reaction to her words. "All you've ever been is my father's henchman." When he turned to glare at her, she glared back. "Oh, you think I don't know what he asked you to do over the years? I'm not that naïve, Ry."

"Things are different now."

"You were never that special to him." She wasn't telling him anything he hadn't probably said to himself over the years. Her father had always made sure his men like Ry were aware of their standing. Her father had drilled into them how they were tools for his use…nothing more.

She went to Ry, slipped her arms around his waist and pressed herself against his back. His muscles were so tense that the ridges felt sharp. "But you've always been that special to me. Don't sacrifice yourself for me when all I want is for you to give yourself to what we can have. We'll protect each other."

"You don't know what you're asking."

"Stop acting like I'm a child. I know what I want. It's you, Ry. It's only ever been you." She'd always had a single-minded determination to be with Ry. Where it came from, she didn't know, but from the moment she'd first seen him, her heart had belonged to Rylan Ward.

She pushed up on tiptoes then kissed the back of his neck. "I want you…only you."

"You can't always get what you want." He turned on her, disentangling her arms, holding her away from his body. "I know that's hard for you to understand, Princess. You don't get to make a demand and get your way with this. You're spoiled, always have been, entitled. You think you can snap your fingers and get what you want. I said no. I mean it. Don't tell me your father never respected me when it's you who has never respected my wishes. At least he was self-aware and upfront about it."

She felt the slap of his words. Her heart shredded right there in her chest. He wanted her. She saw the lust in his eyes, the need for her. She knew that his kisses, every single one they'd shared, were genuine. Yet, he kept pushing her away.

He was scared and a coward, but he wasn't wrong. She'd forced herself on him, time and time again.

She slumped into herself, wrapping her arms around her waist and taking a step back.

He'd said no more times than she could count, and she just kept pushing.

"Fine." She turned away from him, stumbled to the bed, the weight of her guilt heavy on her body. "You want this to end. It's over. I will *never* ask you to be with me again. And I'm sor—" She choked over her words, tears slipping from her eyes. "I'm sorry."

"Good," he said with all the force of his baritone.

One word and it slammed into her body like a knife. She slid onto the bed, tugging the tangled sheets over herself, closed her eyes and wished with everything she had that he would disappear again and leave her to her humiliation.

Chapter Twelve

Everything he'd said the night before had been the truth. Elena had set her sights on him from the time that she had been a teenager and had relentlessly pursued him. He respected her too much to let her fall into the trap of loving him. He was nothing, a dead end. She deserved better. She was right. Her father didn't respect him. He didn't care about Rylan or anything he'd done for the Russio family. He'd exploited Rylan's sense of duty and his dogmatic values and loyalty. What Elena didn't know, and would never know, was that Cai Russio had saved Rylan from a death sentence a week before Elena had met him, and to Rylan, that meant he owed the man, and by proxy, his family, his life.

As much as it sucked to give Elena a dose of brutal honesty, it was what she needed to move on with her life. He was living on borrowed time. His life of violence would catch up with him. He'd die before he'd let any harm come to her, but he'd be damned if he let his feelings for her cloud his judgment and distract him from his job.

He'd gotten caught up in her, romanticized her sacrifice for him. He should have been horrified that she'd put her life on hold because she believed they were meant to be. This wasn't a fairy tale. Nothing good would come from them being together. He was a known entity, and sooner or later, he would die doing this job. He'd reconciled that fact a long time ago. Choices had been made. He'd signed his own death certificate the moment he'd become indebted to Cai.

She hadn't spoken to him as she got up, got ready then sipped at her coffee while glaring out of the window. The sun was blasting heat, and the dark circles under her eyes told him exactly how much sleep she'd gotten.

"I suggest we skip this adventure tour." He knew by the way her spine stiffened that she wouldn't be taking direction from him today.

"You *would* think that."

"Come on, Elena. You're tired. Stay here and rest." He sighed. "Don't be stubborn."

She snorted, downed the rest of her coffee then turned, her eyes surprisingly cool when he was expecting heat. She was always ready for a fight, but her deadpan expression gave him a chill. "You don't get to say anything about me or how I choose to spend my time anymore."

"I do when it comes to your wellbeing, your safety. This adventure tour is an unknown and probably full of ridiculous activities." He shook his head. "It's my job to protect you, even from yourself."

"You're so pompous. You actually think I need you to protect me." She waved her hands to indicate the wide world around them. "I've been doing just fine on my own."

"That's a miracle in and of itself with the way you push things. You're reckless, Elena!"

He hated that she flinched, that he made her regret her past actions toward him. He hated that in order to protect her from him, he had to hurt her.

"I'll make things easy for you." Her expression was neutral—no spark in her eyes to show the depth of her feelings, no quirk to her lips in teasing, no fire at all. "You're fired."

She didn't give him a chance to react. She just moved around him then headed for the door.

He turned to follow her, to stop her from leaving the room without a conversation, but as soon as she opened the door, she was greeted by Sabine, her hand raised, ready to knock.

"Hello, my friend! Are you two ready for the big adventure day?" Sabine beamed. "I can't wait for you to see your game ideas in action! This will be a true testing ground."

Elena looked over her shoulder at him, spearing him with a fuck off and die look before turning back to Sabine, a grin already on her face. "I'm honored that you used my ideas."

"Oh, girl, wait till you see! I'm so excited to hear what you think." Sabine looped her arm around Elena's then tugged her out of the door, leaving Rylan to scramble after them.

* * * *

He didn't know how to get them out of this without making a scene, and as much as it didn't bother him to create a spectacle, something held him back. Maybe it was seeing how genuinely excited Elena was. Her cheeks were flushed, her eyes sparkling, body practically vibrating as they all stood waiting to hear instructions for how the day would go. Maybe it was because he was a coward. Whatever the reason, he stood quietly and listened to the rules of the game, all the while calculating how he'd keep Elena safe. It didn't matter that she'd fired him, even unofficially. He was compelled to protect her, especially from herself.

"I'm sure you've all watched the show *The Incredible Race*." Sabine surveyed the crowd. "Couples will compete through a series of daring tasks that will call on them to work together and balance one another's strengths. Some of these tasks will take you off island for a little excursion fun." She lifted her hand. "Rest assured, security will be keeping tabs, so no one gets lost or hurt."

Rylan moved closer to Elena, letting her know that he was right there. "We need to talk," he said low enough for only her ears. They were *not* going on an excursion.

She pushed back her shoulders then took a few steps forward with her hand up. "Sabine, sorry to interrupt, but I'm wondering if we might shake up the game a bit before we get started."

Sabine grinned over at Elena like they were sharing some kind of private conversation. It made Rylan's shoulders tense more than they already were.

"This should be good!" Sabine clapped, seeming to share Elena's excited vibe. "Go ahead, Elena."

Elena turned to the crowd. "We all know our partners and how they react to stress, but if we're really doing a market test on this game for future clients, then we should be playing with a bit of the unknown, right? Chances are an adventure tour would be with new clients." She waved her hand around the group. "I suggest we swap partners, mix a little work and play. See how we can do as Kitty Cats with quasi strangers."

Maybe this was how Elena did things normally, upping the ante while her boss was laying down the rules. Maybe this was a 'fuck you' to him. Either way, he was not happy about this idea and opened his mouth to object when Sabine beat him to it.

"I love the way your mind works, Elena!" She motioned to the crowd. "Cats, what say you? Are we interested in a swap to truly test out our product?"

The Cats all cheered, and Rylan swore he heard all the men groan. At least, that's what their expressions told him.

Elena caught his eye and smirked. She was putting distance between them, creating a barrier. It would be near impossible for him to keep an eye on her this way.

And yet, he wasn't prepared to ruin her day.

"How secure are these games?" he blurted, calculating the odds of trouble. "What kind of risks are involved?"

"Like I said," Sabine answered with a patronizing smile, "full security at all stops. There are two mainland destinations that all partners will inevitably arrive to. Adam and his team will be monitoring the posts and the water and will be escorting all teams to their destinations and back."

Rylan nodded, knowing he was effectively being told to chill out. He knew security on the island was good, but they'd be leaving at some point and that got his hackles up.

"I'd say it's a go then." Sabine clapped her hands. "Let's shake things up!"

Elena swept past him on her way to another man. "Don't worry, Ry, I won't do anything too risky."

"Hey, partner!" Sonia looped her arm around Ry's. "If we're going to beat Elena at her own game, then we're going to have to play dirty... She doesn't like to lose."

Sabine handed them an orange envelope. "Time starts *now*!"

"And what exactly does that mean?" Rylan watched as Elena chatted animatedly with Sonia's boyfriend, James, and found himself stifling a growl.

"It means that she'll do whatever it takes to win," Sonia said as she tore open the envelope. "Oh shit...this is going to be interesting." She showed him the directions. "I bet some of these games would work better with alliances."

"Well, let's get that sorted first," Rylan said as he beelined for Elena and her new partner. "Hey, James, right?"

The other man had a look of doom on his face as Elena presumably filled him in on her strategies. "Yeah," He looked relieved to shake Ry's hand. "This is nuts. I don't even know how to tie a rope." His gaze skittered to Sonia, his expression pleading for an escape.

Sonia waved him off as she joined them. "Don't be a baby."

"You've got a champ right there." Rylan nodded to Elena. "But I'm an expert on ropes. Why don't we form an alliance to start things off? I know that's what they do on the show, don't they?"

"Fantastic idea, right?" Sonia giggled as she held her hand up. "I thought of it!"

"Brilliant plan!" James said with a clap on Rylan's back before scooping up his girlfriend and kissing her cheek. "That's exactly what they do on the show. You're so smart, baby."

"Makes sense to me," Rylan said with a shrug. "Better to work together, right, Elena? That'll ensure a win for the first round, at least."

All eyes turned to Elena, whose cheeks had taken on a rosy hue while her eyes blasted all kinds of rage. It was easily mistaken for excitement if Sonia's reaction was any indication.

"I'm a smart cookie sometimes, right, El?" Sonia beamed.

"Yep, you sure are." Elena forced a smile through gritted teeth. It all looked painful to Rylan. "Sounds like a plan." She turned her back on them and started toward their first destination. "Let's go. We're wasting time."

And that, as far as Rylan was concerned, was one point for team common sense and zero points for team reckless.

Maybe it would be a fun day after all.

Chapter Thirteen

The first part of the task was learning how to tie ropes, something most Cats knew the basics of, at least, when it came to fun and games. The second part of the task was learning how to get out of them.

Elena was more than annoyed by Ry's alliance. She was furious—a quiet seething that burned. She'd wanted distance from him, but what she got was his hands all over her body as he helped steady her to the pole while the taskmaster, Adam's girlfriend, Sheriff Missy, tied her up with anything but fun and games knots.

"It's surprising how often I've needed this life skill," Missy muttered with a forced laugh.

"The tying-up or untying skill?" Rylan snorted.

"Both," Missy said with a hard tug on Elena's wrists. "Pay attention, Kitty Cat. You never know when you'll *need* to know."

Elena rolled her eyes to hide her true feelings. It should have felt awkward, uncomfortable even, having

Ry there in front of her while she was being bound, but instead, it was all kinds of thrilling. Goosebumps rose and chills zoomed over her from head to toe. Even her pussy clenched like it was expecting something naughty to go down. She cursed her traitorous body for being such a sucker for punishment but kept her mouth shut. She didn't want to scream hysterically at Ry about what an ass he was while at the same time lusting for him to rub his body all over her.

"Now, you've learned about four types of knots," Missy said with one last tug, reminding Elena of the task at hand. "You have exactly two minutes to get yourself out of this one. You can coach your partner with hand directions only. No speaking allowed."

She wagged her finger at them then moved on to the other pairs who were trying to work out of their knot situation.

Elena and Sonia had been the ones tied up—Sonia's damsel-in-distress idea—so it was James and Ry who were coaching. Or, more like Ry, because James was looking at him like he was the god of knots.

Ry's smirk was infuriating but he only had eyes for Sonia, which was also infuriating and quite frankly made Elena's burning fury shift to jealousy. She'd waited a long-ass time for Ry to tie her up, and now that she was, he wasn't even paying attention to her. And worse, she couldn't see the gestures he was using to help Sonia without craning her neck in the most obvious way, and she refused to give him the satisfaction of knowing that she needed him.

James was useless with his hand gestures, presumably emulating Ry without understanding what he was doing. He twisted and turned his wrists as if she could just squirm her way out of the knot. She'd tested its strength, and every move she made seemed to tighten it more. She'd thought that the self-defense training she'd had at her father's insistence would get her out of any bind, but right now, she was blank, her mind empty of any solutions. She couldn't remember the name of this particular knot, but she did recall that she could maneuver in such a way to loosen its bite then wiggle herself free. She just couldn't remember which direction to go. That might have something to do with how hot and bothered she was, and for that, she blamed Ry. If he hadn't been acting like such an ass, she would have been able to stay calm, focus and get herself out of this mess.

She watched Ry with a side eye that was meant to look inconspicuous, but she caught his lip twist and knew he was on to her. He shifted slightly so she could catch him in her peripheral sight and begrudgingly accepted his quiet help. This was, after all, a competition, and she hated to lose.

Ry gestured rotating one wrist then tugging with his fingers. Sonia followed his movements and with a grunt or two, squealed because she was suddenly free. Missy came over in an instant, handing them another envelope, which they huddled together to read. Elena, distracted by how close Sonia and Ry were to one another, lost a good thirty seconds snooping, and James started digging his feet in the dirt like an enraged bull to get her attention back on him.

Elena huffed, her frustration growing. James was frantically trying to show her the way to escape, but his facial expressions were so comical that she couldn't focus on what he was doing. He looked constipated — his eyes scrunched, lips pursed, full concentration mode. She'd laugh if she wasn't so annoyed. She pulled up, flicking her wrists like he showed her but that only tightened the rope enough to make her wince.

"Time is up!" Missy shouted.

Elena sighed, shaking her head. James seemed frustrated as he approached, his hands up as if it were all her fault.

"Great directions," she said with an eye roll.

"It would have helped if you'd been paying attention." He did something quick, tugging on one side of the rope and her hands were free.

She rubbed her sore wrists. *So, this is what defeat feels like.* She didn't like it. "Now what?" Sonia and Ry were gone, disappeared into the trees so Elena couldn't keep any tabs on them.

"Now you wait." Missy held an envelope. "Five-minute time deduction for you two."

This was her game and, in this moment, it sucked balls. *Not in a good way, either.*

Elena slumped onto a boulder, her arms crossed, frustration growing. Yes, it had been her idea to switch up the partners, but she'd done it as punishment to Ry. It wasn't meant to be one for her. And really, she should have been able to master the game with any partner, but she was way too fixated on Ry and what he was doing with Sonia to be of any use to James. Now Ry was gone, frolicking off with Sonia, and she was alone, unprotected…which yes, was totally hypocritical for her to even complain about. She'd wanted him to fight for her—to demand in his Rylan way that she was wrong and that she couldn't fire him. But, much to her shock, he'd gone along with it—which, deep down, made her think that he was right. She was spoiled…entitled. And she did expect to get everything she set her mind on. Until this moment, she hadn't seen a problem with that.

"Sorry I wasn't focused on what you were doing, James." Elena sighed. She didn't like to lose, but she wasn't a sore loser, either, and this wasn't James's fault.

"Ah, that's all right." James settled on the boulder next to her. "I'm not big into games, anyway. And really, if this is a market test for Sabine, a little failure would be good for her to know about, right? Like what do you do about the clients who can't get past the stages successfully?"

Elena's mind snapped into game mode. "You're right, actually. Sitting around kills the buzz completely. We need to have something just as entertaining happening for the losers as we do for the winners." She needed to snap out of sour grapes thinking and focus on how to improve the game. That's what Sabine would value above anyone successfully completing the tour. "Thanks, James. You just inspired me." She gave him a high five, which had him grinning like he was suddenly all into the fun of it.

"Here you two go." Missy handed them their envelope.

Elena stripped the opening to reveal their next task. "Hey, James, what do you say we screw this one up, too?" She showed him the instructions.

"I'd say that'd be way more fun than doing it properly." James laughed as he held his hand for her to take.

Elena took hold so he could heave her to her feet. "Let's fuck this up, partner."

* * * *

They reached their next destination after picking their way through a dense patch of forest. Much to Elena's surprise, Ry and Sonia were still there, struggling to get through the next task.

It was suspicious but not enough to make Elena think that Ry was attempting to hold back from moving on to the next task. It really did look like he was trying his hardest to succeed, but this was not his game and, added bonus, it was entertaining to watch.

Island dancing was tripping him up, and it made Elena giggle at how uncoordinated he was. Surprising too, actually, because he had all the moves when he was licking her — er, defending her from assailants.

Sonia was clearly trying her best to lead but Ry, being Ry, he kept forcing his own moves, which ended up being the wrong ones. Josie, the instructor and judge, watched with an exasperated look on her face.

"This one is not going to be a problem to lose," James whispered, his hand blocking his mouth so only Elena could hear. "I'm so bad at dancing."

"Well, I'm not, so you're going to have to be *really* bad or people are going to realize we're throwing the game." Considering how everyone knew that Elena would do whatever she needed to do to win, her losses had to be believable. "Be super bad."

"That, I can definitely do." James smiled at Josie, who had just finished her final judgment of Sonia and Rylan.

"That was painful," Josie said with a grin. She was a Kitty Cat who'd been with Sabine for a very long time — definitely huge competition for Elena when it came to getting their boss's praise. "I hope you two are better at following directions." She didn't want to make it seem like Josie was bad at her job, instructing these speedy dance lessons, so whatever James did had to be spectacularly obvious that it was his fault entirely.

Elena watched Ry and Sonia step over to one of the seating areas looking dejected.

Another snafu in their plan was that Ry knew Elena had taken dancing lessons from the time that she was a child. It was a complication that would demand she put her best effort into making it look like she was trying to win. She just hoped James was as bad as he said he was.

Josie took them through the dance, which was all hip rolling, quick steps and definitely required a sense of timing. James wasn't lying when he said he couldn't do any of those things. He was bad, so bad that Elena had to wonder if she could lead him to success if he was a client. She suspected that even Josie would have a hard time teaching James rhythm. He moved his arms awkwardly, making him look like a robot malfunctioning. His feet seemed to get in the way, no matter how she tried to guide him, and his timing was…well, awful. What he was good at, which was a relief to know for Sonia's sake, was the hip rolling sequence. The man could gyrate like the best of them. The problem was more about his confidence, which seemed insurmountable.

They gave it three worst shots. Elena did what she could so it looked real, leading without being pushy, smiling encouragingly and laughing when James stepped on her feet over and over or when they bumped heads because he went the wrong way on a turn. Ultimately in less than ten minutes, they failed to meet Josie's requirements.

"Fifteen-minute time delay," Josie said with an exaggerated frown. "You're stuck here with them." She nodded toward Sonia and Ry, who had five minutes left on their time delay, then moved on to the next two couples who had come to do the challenge.

"That was rough," Ry said as to James. "I feel your pain, man."

"Yeah, not my partner's fault, though." James grinned at Elena. "You've got killer moves, lady."

"Don't we all?" Sonia said with a sigh. "Come sit next to me, girlfriend." She patted the space next to her. "Let's wallow in our failure."

"I have a better idea," Elena said. "How about we kill the time with our own game?"

"What do you have in mind?" Sonia perked up.

Rylan narrowed his eyes. "What kind of game?"

Chapter Fourteen

They played twenty-questions, a game that Rylan had never experienced before. Of course, Elena had made it a naughty version so the questions that got asked were all borderline pornographic.

"How wet is it?"

"Harder than a steel rod?"

"Does it taste salty?"

"At least eight inches?"

"Wider than a sausage?"

"Would it fit in my mouth?"

He'd been both hot *and* bothered, and his mind had taken him to dangerous territory, wanting to drag Elena into a cluster of bushes and have his way with her.

Yes, it's hard, thick and aching for you.

He didn't want to leave Elena with James once their time was up and they were told to move onto the next challenge ahead of the others, not when her mind was in the gutter and she'd dragged all of them there with her.

He hated being separated from her even for ten minutes.

Despite the island being safe and no dangers lurking, he wanted to be close to Elena, which was hugely problematic because he knew it had nothing to do with duty or obligation. He didn't want to miss out on her voice, laugh, essence, and it bothered him at a gut level that she didn't seem bothered at all that he was leaving.

He still couldn't believe that she'd been mad enough to fire him.

That feeling was confusing as hell because he'd meant it when he'd told Elena to give it up. He'd wanted her to stop pursuing him — or at least, that's what he'd been telling himself as he said it, knowing that it was for her own good that he was pushing her away. Now it was like a hot poker needling him to fix it — to make her run after him, demand his attention, crave him like she always seemed to be.

Yeah, I'm a shithead.

If he was going to do a psychological deep dive, then he had to be honest about why he did what he did. He'd pushed her away because he was scared.

If he gave in to her, he'd be lost to her. If he was lost to her, he'd never be able to do his job properly. He'd take a bullet for her, absolutely, a thousand times over, but he didn't want to be so reckless that he lost his life in the process. He wanted her…always had.

Sonia had him moving to the next challenge, and when he realized what they'd be doing, he wished he'd tied Elena up for real and kept her in their suite for the day. There was a huge gameboard laid out with multiple colored cat heads of red, yellow, green and blue.

Twister, Kitty Cat style.

Just fucking wonderful.

The two couples ahead of them finished up the game with one pair moving on and one staying behind to watch Rylan's humiliation. He was not comfortable getting handsy with Sonia. He was not okay with bending his body in compromising poses. He hated everything about this.

"Let's do it, partner!" Sonia clapped her hands, jumping on the balls of her feet like she was revved up with a blast of accelerant.

"You have to wait for Elena and James to catch up. They'll be your partners for this one." Sabine motioned to the board. "But we'll consider this a warm up. Get on the board. Let's see how you two move."

"Oh, we've got moves. Right, Rylan?" Sonia grabbed his arm and tugged him forward. "Take your shoes off, and let's get this party started!"

Expectation was a bitch at the best of times, but with all eyes on him, Rylan didn't want to ruin everyone's buzz. Or at least, that's what he was telling himself as he let Sonia pull him forward. What he was really thinking was to meet fire with fire. Elena was playing her own version of a game, and he suddenly had the urge to play right back. Let her see him all tangled up with Sonia. Maybe that would get her to rethink his termination.

By the time Elena showed up, Rylan was wrapped around Sonia, sweating in his discomfort, because, really, Sonia was just as twisted as Elena when it came to supposed fun, and he was wishing he could be anywhere but where he was.

"Your man has some moves, El," Sabine said with a laugh. "He's been getting all up in Sonia's business." She acted like she was whispering, cupping her hand to cover her mouth as Elena approached but loud enough for everyone to hear. "Probably wishing it was you."

Elena took the scene in, her eyes narrowing on the center of the board. Rylan's one arm was wrapped around Sonia's waist, one leg between hers, stuck in a position that was both difficult and awkward. Her eyes narrowed farther. Her lips pouted. She shifted one hand to her hip, the other stroking her jaw. He knew that look. He'd seen it a million times on Elena's face over the years when she didn't get what she wanted.

She was jealous. Something surged through him that felt like electricity, a zap of triumph. She was absolutely jealous!

To test it out, Rylan's next move put his face so close to Sonia's that he could kiss her without moving an inch. He didn't flinch or pull away. He leaned in, getting so close that all Sonia had to do was sway and their lips would touch. A quick glance at Elena told him everything he needed to know. She was locked in on them, her eyebrows furrowed, lips curled down. She didn't like this any more than he did.

A flash that he recognized as Elena-style determination crossed her face and her expression changed. She met his gaze head on then kicked her sandals off.

She got on the game board and immediately maneuvered herself closer to him. She was so damn flexible that she curled herself up like a pretzel, her arms crossed around one of his legs and her ass in his face, taunting him so badly that he wanted to take a bite just to leave a mark.

Sabine hooted. Others catcalled.

James grunted through his own torture on the other side of the body tangle.

Rylan's next move had him sliding himself under Elena so his chest brushed up against hers. Her tits dangled enough to torment him as he limboed carefully beneath her arched body. Why was he doing this? For her sake? Or for his own? At some point he'd lost the plot of his own game.

Elena locked eyes with him as their bodies touched, her breath coming out in short pants. His cock was hard, aching, her nipples beaded, poking through the fabric of her tank. Her skin glistened with sweat, and he had to hold his breath to keep his senses clear of her intoxicating scent. He wanted to lick her collarbone. He wanted to grind his dick against her hip. He wanted to give up control, wrap his arms around her waist and pull her into his body.

He was stuck with Elena practically on top of him and his mind whirling through all the possible ways they could do this exact move in bed with far more satisfying results.

"Don't look at me like that," she said, her voice husky and low. "You're not thinking friend-zone thoughts."

She was right. He wasn't. And the fact that he was now in the friend zone had his body doing all kinds of rebellious things. His cock pulsed so hard that he was sure everyone could see the twitching through his shorts, and his heart? Well, it did a nosedive into his gut.

He was fucked—or wanted to be, at least.

As if she could read his body, Elena lowered closer to his torso, bringing her body heat to envelop him as she shifted one leg so that her thigh brushed ever so slightly against his raging cock.

And that was just about all he could take. He collapsed, one arm around her waist to drag her down with him. They landed with a thud, her body pressed against his, her thigh still wedged snuggly into his crotch, her lips right there, waiting for punishment.

He couldn't do it. No man could endure this—not without blue balls the size of watermelons. He wouldn't deny himself for a moment longer.

He kissed her, took her lips, sucked her tongue and demanded she pay up for all the years of torment she'd put him through. *Fuck it.* He couldn't push her away anymore.

"You're losing this game," he said as he broke their kiss. He didn't give her a chance to argue. He scrambled to his feet, heaving her along with him until she was in his arms, trapped by his embrace. "And we're going to the room to finish what you started."

Chapter Fifteen

"You drive me insane," Rylan growled as he nuzzled her throat, his hands splayed over her ass. "This is not good for either of us."

"It is, though, and you know it is, so quit being yourself for half a second and let it happen." She was breathless, practically panting, and he wanted more.

Quit being himself? Right. That's exactly what he needed to do. He needed to get lost in her, finally, to let himself go. *Fuck it.* This felt too good to stop.

She knew the second he gave in to her because she grinned against his lips and slid her hands up his back, pressing her lush body closer to his.

He walked her backward until her legs hit the bed, but she didn't fall. Instead, she dropped, ripping her lips away from his so suddenly that he wanted to chase after her. When he saw her intention, on her knees, hands working his belt, he stopped overthinking. Stopped thinking...period.

His cock strained against his pants, eager for her hands, her mouth, and there was no way he would do anything to stop this from happening. He'd fantasized about this very moment, how she'd look as she took his cock for the first time with her plump lips, holding him hostage in her wet mouth.

She stroked his shaft through the fabric of his pants, and he groaned, wanting her to get on with it but also dying for her to take her time.

To torture him.

She looked up at him through her dark lashes, licked her lips and killed him with seduction. She was so beautiful...always had been. Her body was lush. His cock pulsed. It wept. It begged for her mouth.

She grinned then ripped his zipper down and, as his dick slipped out of the opening, she was on him, her hot breath rolling over his head seconds before he was encased between her lips, stretching her pretty mouth as she took him down.

His thoughts exploded into a million stars. His body swayed closer. He laid his hand on her head to steady himself, to get his bearings.

It was no use, though. She was everything he needed, wanted, was desperate for and if that didn't rock a person's foundation, then nothing would.

He was shaken right to his core. His heart swelled, dipped low then high. His body coiled, pleasure overruling everything else.

She kneaded his balls softly, sending pulses through him that made his knees buckle again and again. A moan vibrated through him, and she returned the vibration with her own moan that rolled over his dick, shooting sensation to every erogenous zone he had.

He gripped her hair, guiding her over his cock as she attempted to take him down her throat, choking a little as she accommodated him perfectly. They fit together like this, and he knew they'd fit together in other ways, too.

Ry let her go for longer than he thought he could handle. Her movements were slow, leisurely stroking and sucking until he was too amped up to take another lick. His cock was ready to blow, and he wanted to be inside her when it did.

He pulled her head back then coaxed her up, leaving his dick to bob in the cool air, torturing him more, then kissed her like he'd always wanted to, sucking her lips, pumping her mouth, stroking her tongue. She fell against him, weaving her fingers through his hair, pulling him down as she fell backward, taking them both to the bed so his weight was on her, his cock abrading against her shorts.

Her clothes needed to come off, *now*. He broke their kiss, then trapped her hands, wrists clasped in one of his hands when she tried to pull him back. He kissed her jaw, nipped at her earlobe, made her sigh and shudder as he moved down her body. He yanked her tank top up, desperate to get to her tits. She tugged on her wrists, and he let her go, giving her room to help him strip her clothes off. His lips never left her skin as she shimmied out of her shorts. He slipped down her body, kissing his way along her stomach while she yanked her tank top and bra off, giving him access to everything she had.

He parted her legs, one hand on the inside of her thigh, the other on her breast, cupping her tit so it spilled from his palm, her nipple a hard little point that he couldn't resist flicking.

Her scent rolled over his tongue. After his first taste the other day, he wanted nothing more than to eat her again. She was luscious, her pussy lips plump, wet, delicious. As he licked her slit, she cried out, so he did it again.

She teased her other nipple and rolled her hips up, begging with her body to give her what she needed. He was in no mood to deny that. He kissed her clit, a tender touch before sucking the little nub into his mouth, stroking it hard with his tongue. She bucked, her legs quivered, and he savored the torture.

His cock was harder than steel, rubbing along the edge of the mattress as he stroked her clit. Just the barest touch on his crown was enough to make cum dribble.

He'd waited too long. Forcing himself to keep distance between them had been foolish. The days of denying himself were over. Elena was ready, her pussy open, waiting for him to fuck her.

He pulled back, got his bearings, his head in the clouds as he stared down the length of her body. She watched him through hooded lids, her teeth pinching her bottom lip, so incredibly sexy as she spread her legs wide, inviting him to sink into her cushion.

He wiped his mouth, then moved up her body like a predator hunting. He caged her in his arms until they were face to face once again, her tits pressed against his chest, her hands on his ass, moving her legs to wrap around his hips. He poked and prodded her pussy, his cock on a hair-trigger, aching to drill her hard and fast. Instead, he eased in slowly, savoring every second of penetration.

She was heaven.

He shivered.

She was *his*.

She held his stare, her eyes locked on his, her lips parted, her breath coming out in short pants. He was stretching her open, and her tight little pussy sucked him in deeper, coaxing him to push harder. She wrapped her legs around him tightly, tugging him closer. He kept going, sinking into her even though it seemed impossible that he'd fit all the way inside.

But she took him to the hilt, and as he lay there, settled in her pussy, he couldn't believe he was finally getting what he most wanted. *My Elena.*

She tilted her face up, pressing closer then kissed his throat. "Fuck me, Ry."

Her words snapped any remaining restraint. His mind dissolved into need and want. What she wanted. What he needed.

He pulled out then thrust back with everything he had, drilling her hard, fast — relentlessly pounding into her rolling hips, her arching body, meeting his every move. She moaned, gripped his ass tighter, whispered against his skin that she wanted more.

They fucked like wild animals who couldn't get enough. He flipped her over and filled her from behind, cupping her dangling breasts and teasing her nipples. Sweat dripped onto her back, mingling with hers until they were both slick, riding through the thrusting, pumping, until his balls got tight, and his dick screamed. Her pussy clenched hard, pulsating around his cock.

He was on the edge, desperate to come but just as desperate to keep going. He'd never get enough of her.

She came with a scream, his name on her lips, and he followed her, jets of hot cum coating her pussy walls.

The pleasure shot him out of his body, so he felt like he was flying, soaring into outer space.

He thrust until he had nothing left, draining every drop he had, every pulse of his cock. Her legs gave way. They collapsed into a heap of tangled arms and legs. She curled herself into his chest — her back to his front, her body heaving as she caught her breath.

As he floated back to her, his nerve endings sparking with residual pleasure, he wrapped one arm around her waist then kissed her shoulder.

"Best idea ever," Ry said, his voice dreamy and far away.

Elena laughed softly. "Told ya so."

Chapter Sixteen

Waking up in Ry's arms was definitely the best vacation Elena had ever had. She didn't want to move and rouse him, but she couldn't help tilting her head to watch him while he slept—something she'd never seen in real life. In fact, for years, she'd felt that he had to be superhuman and didn't need sleep. All the times he'd guarded her, he'd been awake at all hours, and she'd know because she made it a point to check—which had vexed him something awful, her showing up in the middle of the night, waltzing into the kitchen claiming that she needed a drink or a snack when really she was checking to see if he'd dozed off. She'd never once caught him snoozing, but she did quite enjoy how his brow furrowed and his jaw tightened to see her out of bed and walking around in carefully chosen lingerie for his eyes only.

"You're staring at me," he mumbled, his lip quirking on one side. "It's creepy."

She swatted him on the chest and laughed. "Just admiring." She truly couldn't believe they were here, together, finally.

He smiled then, his eyes still closed as he tightened his grip on her, pulling her close so he could kiss her forehead. It flooded her with warmth, not like the lust she normally felt toward him, which was blazing hot. This was more like a hug she didn't know she needed. It felt right, like all the pieces of her had come together with a glue she didn't know existed. She loved it. She loved him…his essence. They were meant to be like this. She'd always known.

Yet, for true love, it had taken a damn long time to get to this moment.

She pulled back to ogle him some more and her gaze snagged on the scar that stretched across his cheek, down his jaw almost to his throat. She touched it with fingertips, so gentle that he sighed, then nuzzled into her hair.

"I've been such a pain in the ass," she said, her hand lingering on his jaw. "Truly a brat."

"Yes," he said then laughed when she swatted his chest again. He gripped her fingers, entwining theirs together. "Scars come with the job."

She'd noticed. He had evidence of injury all over his body, some looking fiercer than others and all a reminder of the sacrifices he'd made for her family. "That one was my fault, though."

"Nah, it was the guy with the knife who holds all the blame on that one." Ry lifted her hand to his lips then kissed her palm.

Again, she melted as her body soaked up his tenderness.

She'd distracted him the night he'd gotten that injury. Lying in his bed, barely clothed, waiting for him to come to bed after he'd done his rounds, not realizing of course that he would never sleep when he was on duty. After over an hour of waiting, she'd taken matters to the next level—young, dumb and looking for trouble.

Elena screamed. "Rylan, come quick! I need you!" Then she fell into the bed in a fit of giggles, knowing that Ry would batter down the walls to get to her if she thought she needed rescuing.

When he did just that, slamming into his bedroom with the wildest look in his eyes, she felt triumphant. He took her in, scorching her from head to toe then back again, his gaze halting at the gauzy see-through material over her breasts, the lace barely covering her pussy and all the curves in between.

"Elena, damn it…" He rubbed his hand over his face. "This isn't a game." But his eyes said he liked what he saw. He really *liked what he saw. She crooked her finger and beckoned him to her. He took a step closer to the bed almost like she was pulling him with an invisible string. "I have a job to do."*

That wasn't a no.

She slithered off the bed, making sure to showcase all her assets. She had him on the hook. She just needed to reel him in. Tonight, finally, she'd have her prize.

He met her halfway, another good sign.

"We can't—"

But she was already moving up his body, gliding her hands along his muscles that were hidden under his suit. He was built like a mythic hero from a romance novel with ridges and divots that she wanted to explore…with her tongue.

She propped herself up so her tits crushed against his chest then nibbled on his chin, kissing the stubble along his jaw. "We can."

He sighed a deep shuddering explosion of breath, and she knew she'd won. He was giving in, finally.

She kissed her way to his lips then waited. She wanted him to make the move, to truly give her what she knew they both wanted. She pressed herself closer, angling her hips so that they fit like they would if he were on top of her, pressing down, ready to fuck her brains out.

"Ry – "

He yanked her head, his fingers tangled in her hair, then closed his lips onto hers. It was electric, on fire, and she simmered with each swipe of his tongue, each probing lick. His lips were firm, intense, relentless, everything she'd ever imagined and more…so much more. It lasted for an eternity and only for a second. When he pulled away, she couldn't breathe. She wanted more.

She took a few steps back, coaxing him by crooking her finger at the same time that she rubbed her hand along the curve of her breast, down her waist to her hips. His eyes were riveted the whole way.

She made it to the bed then climbed on, turning her back for seconds, and when she looked over her shoulder, she saw what he couldn't.

A shadow loomed behind him, moving stealthy. She opened her mouth but no scream came out. Ry frowned, took another step toward her and that's what saved his life, because the knife came across his face instead of his throat.

Blood gushed and Ry spun, using his forearms to knock the assassin back into the hall, where he disappeared into the shadows.

The door slammed, kicked by Ry on his way out. Elena sat stunned. Her stomach twisted and bile rose. She'd never truly believed that they were in danger. She'd never taken the *threats seriously because nothing had ever come from them. She realized in that moment that nothing had ever happened because Ry had made sure it wouldn't.*

The door shook, rattling as something heavy slammed into it. Elena heard grunting, yelling, a loud thump again on the door. She was frozen on the bed, too terrified to do anything but pray that Ry was winning the fight. She couldn't lose him. He was the love of her life, even if he didn't realize it yet.

"Hey, El, don't get caught up in the past." Ry tilted her chin up, his eyes open, soaked with the same tenderness that she felt in his touch. "It wasn't your fault."

He knew she blamed herself. She'd repeated the same mantra to him for months after the attack. *I'm sorry. It's my fault.* He'd always told her that she needed to get past that.

He was right. She did.

She pushed back, then looped her leg over his hips. She had him right where she wanted him now. She'd show him how grateful she was for him being in her life.

He stared up at her, his eyelids hooded, lips slightly parted. She nuzzled her pussy against his cock, slicking it with her heat.

"I could get used to this." He gripped her hips, rocking her along his shaft.

"You should get used to it." She leaned down so her hair brushed against his face, her lips almost touching his. "I'm not going anywhere." She kissed him softly. "And neither are you."

He smiled, and it made her heart skip a beat. No frown. No pulling away. That was all done. He was hers now. She knew it. He knew it.

"Come here," he growled as he latched his hand to the back of her neck then brought her down for a proper kiss.

She rocked her hips as he sucked her mouth, pumping her the way she wanted to pump him. Without breaking their kiss, she slipped her hand between them then slid his cock home. They both groaned, melting into one another.

A frenzy took hold of her heart, her soul, her body unable to get enough of his touch, his kiss, the way his cock stretched her out and filled her up. He cupped her tits, and she pulled back, riding him with abandon, arching her back and moaning to the ceiling as she let him see what he did to her.

"You're so beautiful, El," he said, his hips moving in time with hers. "I've been such a fool."

She smiled to herself before tilting her head back so she could look down at him. "And don't you forget it."

She playfully smacked his chest and he, in turn, tweaked her nipples hard enough to make her cry out. Then, with a sly wink, he rolled her over onto her back, her legs splayed wide, his hands cupping her ass as he drilled her hard, fast and relentlessly.

She came with earthquake shudders, riding out every thrust he gave, his muscles flexing, releasing, until he spewed his load so deep inside that she felt him coat every part of her.

This was so long overdue that she couldn't get enough. He was everything—a drug, a balm. More than that, he was hers and she was his.

How will I leave this bed now that I have him right where I want him?

Problems for later.

She sighed as he collapsed next to her, taking up his now usual spot at her side, curling his body along hers so they were touching in every way. He kissed behind her ear as he tried to settle his breathing.

"I'm going to need some sleep before we can do that again." He sighed like sleep was such a disappointment, and it made her heart flutter like a wild bird's.

"*I'm* going to need some sleep if I'm going to be in any way coherent for my big meeting with Sabine in a few hours." By the way the moon shone, they'd fucked most of the night away. "You're not going to tell me to forget it, are you?"

"Nah, you do you." He nuzzled against her neck, his breath deeper, heavier. "Technically though, you are a multi-millionaire. Your father showed me the papers, effective upon his death. You don't need a promotion or, for that matter, a job. You're filthy rich."

A multi-millionaire. A sickening lump settled in her stomach.

"What do you mean?" Her voice was barely a croak.

His answering snore told her nothing and everything at the same time. To Ry, it was inevitable. Her father was dead, so she inherited everything. To her, it was not. Her father had broken his word. He'd vowed to cut her out, just as she'd wanted, on the day she'd left him forever.

Her world tilted sideways as she fell through the mattress to the hard truth of Ry's words. "*Showed me the papers…effective upon his death.*"

She was the sole heir to her father's bloody dynasty.

Chapter Seventeen

Elena was at her meeting with Sabine, and Rylan had some thinking to do.

He'd crossed a line many times over the last few hours with Elena. and he didn't regret it. How could he? She was everything he'd fantasized she'd be, and having her under him — hell, on top, to the side, pressed up against a wall, screaming for him to fuck her — was something he didn't want to give up. And it wasn't just the physical aspect of their relationship shift, either. His heart felt full for the first time maybe in his life. She'd always had a place in there, hidden away, easy to deny, but giving in to his desire had awakened that part of his heart with a ferocity that couldn't be ignored.

So, he had to figure out a way to keep her in his life, and that meant staying alive…no unnecessary risks. He also needed to plan how to do that with Elena staying at Cowan Enterprises. She'd worked hard for everything she'd earned, and the promotion Rylan knew she was getting at this very moment was well deserved. He couldn't take that away from her. He couldn't expect her to live in hiding.

Which meant he had to make a call.

"Hey, Ryyyy… How's it hanging, dude?" Chip Wilson, one of Ry's only friends—more like a brother really—always answered like he'd just come home after a binge-drinking rodeo. His voice was raspy and his volume too loud.

"Chip, what's the status?"

"Well, hello to you, too!" Chip clicked away on his computer, no doubt already searching for what Rylan wanted. "Where'd you disappear to, my man? You fell off the radar these last few days."

Rylan only used burners that he discarded regularly, because he knew Chip, along with many of his hacker counterparts, could track him easily with a device that stayed with him for too long. Not that he didn't want Chip knowing where he was… He trusted the man with his life and then some, but if Chip could find him, so could others, and the bad guys had a Chip of their own working for them.

"I'm on vacation."

Chip sucked in a breath. "Dudddddde," he said on the exhale. "Did you just swear at me?" He laughed a full belly laugh. "Did you just say you're on vacation? Is that code for something? You in trouble? Want me to send the cavalry?"

"Not necessary and yes, I am actually on vacation—a forced one…with Elena. I'm protecting her, remember?"

"Protecting her in all the ways she wants, I hope." Chip laughed again. "Now that I think about it, you do sound very satisfied, my man. She finally get her way with you? That girl is something—"

"I'm not calling to chit chat," Rylan interrupted. Chip knew about Elena's single-minded drive to get Rylan in bed and ultimately into her life. He'd always been team Elena, giving Rylan shit for denying such a beautiful woman like he had been. "I need to know where we stand."

"Yeah, yeah. You know I'm on it." Chip clicked some more on his keyboard. "The chatter is quiet."

"Quiet as in 'a plan is in motion' or quiet as in 'they can't find her'?"

"They can't find her. The bounty on her head has doubled, but they know you're with her, so only a few guys are on it." He sighed. "You're going to need to make her disappear."

"That's the problem. She's built a life with these people. I need to figure out a way to make it safe." Rylan felt none of the usual hesitation in saying those words, no screaming in his gut that it was wrong. Elena had created a world for herself, and he wanted to be in it, with her, safely.

"Ah shit, you did sleep with her!" Chip whistled. "About fucking time, dude. Congratulations!"

"Chip," Rylan growled.

"Okay, okay, sheesh!" Chip typed. "Well, Cowan Enterprises is pretty secure. They've had a few incidents over the years, but they also have connections. Not many assassins will come for her while she's under Sabine Cowan's watch. That woman is scary as fuck. I'd say the closer Elena can get to her boss, the better. No one touches Sabine."

Elena's promotion might just make her more protected than she was before. The upper echelon of Sabine's employees must have better security if Chip's theory was right.

"You think you can find a way to make it work?" Just in case she didn't get the promotion, Rylan wanted her to keep the life she loved. "With me here full time?"

"Dude!" His voice softened. "Awww, man, you're in for the long haul. It's about time. Elena is a catch, and you're lucky she didn't give up on you."

"Chip." He sighed. "This is serious."

"Isn't it always?" Chip paused long enough to make Rylan think the line had disconnected. "Yeah, I can find a way. Give me some time. I'll figure something out."

* * * *

"I can't tell you how grateful I am, Sabine." Elena nearly choked on her next words, her heart in her throat, palms sweaty. "But I can't take the promotion." She rushed through the rest because there was no way she could give herself a second to take it back. "And I'm handing in my resignation." Well, not actually. It was typed on her phone and she'd sent it to Sabine's email as she said those words out loud, but there wasn't anything official to hand over—just her broken heart.

"I don't accept." Sabine shook her head, her smile only wavering slightly. "You are a valuable member of our team, and I want you as a leader. What can I do to sweeten the deal? Ten percent signing bonus? Twenty? An extra three weeks' vacation time?" She put her hands on her knees then leaned forward. "Name your price."

She was dressed in a white sundress that showcased her tanned skin and healthy glow, an outfit far more casual than Elena had seen her boss in before this trip. It was a carefree side of Sabine that Elena really loved. She looked like she was on vacation.

Elena almost wished Sabine was in one of her power suits, all business. It would maybe make this whole situation a little more official and less heartbreaking.

Probably not, though. The slow cuts to her soul were tearing her up, and she could only hope she didn't bleed to death before she got all the words out that she needed to say.

It was torture, but it was necessary. She'd been childish to think she could continue with her life now that she was the sole heir to her father's blood fortune. She'd been too entitled to believe she could walk away from her past.

While she couldn't do anything about her father breaking his vow to disinherit her, she could do something to diffuse the immediate threat. Ry was right. She had a target on her back now more than ever, and she couldn't risk the safety of everyone she cared about.

"It's not you—"

"Don't give me that" —Sabine had her hand up to stop Elena from speaking—"'it's not you it's me' shit. Spill it. What's going on?" She pointed toward the door. "Does it have anything to do with your fiancé showing up all of a sudden? Is he taking issue with your work? If he is, I'd like to have a word, because—"

"No, no!" Elena tried to laugh off Sabine's sudden mama bear rage, but deep down she felt like she needed that kind of reminder that she was valued and loved for who she was...or at least, who they *thought* she was. "I haven't been exactly honest with you...about me...my background." *My baggage.* "My family."

Sabine closed her mouth then sat back, resting her hands on her thighs as if she were prepared to listen until the end of time to whatever Elena had to say.

"Rylan isn't my fiancé." Elena knew she had to start somewhere, so she latched onto the most obvious. "*Yet.* I mean, not for lack of trying on my part."

"You're crazy about him. That's obvious."

"I am, for as long as I can remember. But until recently"—Elena felt her cheeks heat—"we haven't exactly been a couple...or even together, together."

Sabine nodded as if she totally understood, when Elena knew it was impossible for her to guess the reality of her life, her past, who her family was.

"He's always been an important part of my life, though." Vitally important. "And he needs me to leave with him as soon as this trip is done."

"Leave to where?"

"I can't tell you, and I don't know for how long." She twisted her hands on her lap. "But it'll be a while...maybe forever. So, I can't say I'll be on the team when I don't even know if I'll be physically around for a long time. And I'm sorry...so, so sorry, because I wanted the promotion more than you can know. I've worked so hard for it." Her voice wavered. She clenched her fists and fought tears. "But my life, my past, has caught up to me, and I can't put anyone in dang—" She gulped back those words and covered them up with others. "I can't get you tangled up in my messy history."

Sabine didn't say anything at first. She held Elena's stare until Elena couldn't take it anymore.

"I'm sorry," she said again.

Sabine didn't console her. She didn't even tell her not to worry. Instead, she narrowed her eyes in a classic 'Sabine is deeply thinking' expression.

"I wish things could be different." Elena patted her legs, a nervous twitch that made her feel silly and started to get up, knowing that she was a giant disappointment to Sabine. "Ry and I can leave today if you'd rather us not be here."

Sabine sighed as she brought her fingers to her temple and rubbed an ache Elena knew she'd caused. "And, I gather, you won't tell me what this messy history entails?"

Elena shook her head.

"And if I ask Rylan?"

"He won't tell you, either. But please know that he has my best interests at heart. He's doing what he's doing to protect me."

"Is there any danger to the other Cats? To any of us here?" Even without Elena saying, Sabine must have guessed that whatever was dragging her away was not a silly reason.

"No…but there might be. That's why I have to go away — at least until the danger dies down." Part of her died saying those words, but another part of her, a tiny spark of hope, gave her the courage to stand tall. She would be with Ry. He would fill her heart and repair the damage leaving this job was causing.

"In my experience, danger doesn't usually die down when you're a magnet for it. You've got to face it head on." Sabine sighed as she stood. "I don't want you to cut your vacation short, but I understand why you need to leave. Join us tonight for dinner. It was supposed to be a celebration of your promotion, but instead it'll be a farewell for now." She held her hand out, then changed her mind and tugged Elena into her arms for a hug. "You will always have a place in my company and in the Cat family, no matter how long you're gone."

Chapter Eighteen

Rylan had done the one thing he said he wouldn't do, and that was to put Elena in a situation of possible risk. He was making an exception because she'd been so devastated when she'd returned from her meeting with Sabine. She'd been on the verge of tears, and it had been obvious that she was fighting to keep herself calm. He'd wanted to hug her, to tell her it would be okay, but she'd hidden away in the bathroom for a while and he'd given her space to mourn.

When she'd come out a half hour later, her makeup was refreshed, her hair done in a springy ponytail and she was smiling…a smile that didn't reach her eyes but was a signal to him that she wasn't going to rehash the details with him.

"My father broke his vow to disinherit me, and now I have to pay for it."

She hadn't said anything beyond that, but Rylan understood. Cai had told her she'd be free to live her life, that he wouldn't burden her with family trouble.

What that had meant to her and what that had meant to him were two different things. Elena hadn't known there was an expiration date on her freedom.

Rylan hadn't expected her to give it all up—not once he realized how much it meant to her to be part of the Cowan team, not when he fully came to understand how hard she'd worked. She ended her relationship with the Cats, and he knew it was to save them from possible danger. She'd quit, even though Rylan knew it was shredding her heart to pieces.

"You sure this is what you want?" He had to shout a little to be heard above the noise of the boat they were on, racing toward the mainland for dinner with the upper echelon of Cowan Enterprises.

Wind whipped Elena's ponytail. She looked majestic as her green sundress billowed around her.

Elena wrapped her arms around him, nestling into his side where she belonged. "I'm sure. I can't put anyone else in danger. It was silly for me to think my life would just go on being the same now that I'm the only one left."

Not silly, he wanted to say, but instead, he kissed the top of her head and squeezed her closer.

They were leaving that night, right after the dinner that had been planned to celebrate her promotion. Apparently, Sabine's assistant Cammie was coming on the private jet with two other Cowan Enterprises couples who'd had to delay their vacation in order to wrap up some work. After dinner was over, Rylan and Elena would leave on that same jet. Destination…South America, where Rylan's safe house awaited.

"It doesn't have to be forever, El." He nestled his chin onto the top of her head, and she leaned into him, sculpting to his body like she was part of him.

He felt her take a shuddering breath.

"We both know it does."

He still had Chip working on a plan, and he hoped the security savant would figure something out so he could give Elena what she wanted in the end.

For now, though, they'd go along with her plan...dinner then disappear. There could be worse things. Rylan had made sure the safe house was filled with every amenity he could think of to make Elena's life comfortable. They'd be together...safe.

Knowing that it came at the cost of Elena's ultimate happiness was a buzzkill of the biggest kind. Would she accept it with time? *Probably*. Would he be able to live without trying to find a way to make it work here for her? *No*.

They docked right at the restaurant that they were eating at. As Rylan helped Elena out of the boat without both of them ending up in the water — a tricky maneuver to say the least — he took a quick scan of the surroundings. The restaurant itself was up a flight of steep stairs, sitting on an overhang with huge columns supporting the deck where he could make out a group of people milling around.

"We have the whole place," Adam said as he moved in next to Rylan. "Security on every door."

"Lots of windows." Rylan commented.

Adam nodded. "That there are."

Rylan took mental note of the surrounding land. A sharpshooter might have a target if Elena hugged the east side of the deck, but otherwise, there didn't seem to be any access points that weren't covered by a hulking guard. A drone would be spotted, especially with the security Rylan could see walking the perimeter of the deck. Anything or anyone who approached the restaurant would stick out.

Satisfied that she'd be safe for the duration of the meal, Rylan offered his arm and together they made their way up the stairs.

The party seemed to be just getting started, with clusters of people milling around, drinks in hand, laughing, talking, hugging.

"Elena, Sabine filled me in." A woman wearing a black-and-white skintight dress pulled Elena into an embrace, three men standing like a semi-circle around her. "I can't believe you're leaving."

"It's okay, Viv. It's what needs to happen," Elena said as she pulled herself out of Viv's arms.

Viv's eyes sparkled with unshed tears. "I get it. I do. I had plans for us...big ideas. I'm going to miss you so much!" She sighed. "And I supposed this is the man who's to blame." She smiled as she turned her accusing eyes toward Rylan. She wasn't being hateful or mean, but Rylan could tell that Elena's departure would be a huge loss for Viv. "You're the love of Elena's life, I presume? I'm Vivian, and these are my partners." She nodded behind her to the three men standing sentry. "I'd say it's nice to meet you, but really, I'm so bummed that you're taking Elena away from us."

He smiled back, knowing that her words were that of a good friend. Elena had people here...another reason that she had to stay. She was adored by her coworkers. Finding that kind of friend group was hard. Walking away from it was going to kill Elena's soul. "Unfortunately I am, but I'm hoping it'll be temporary."

Elena didn't bother acknowledging Rylan's comment. Instead she walked with Viv to another couple, a tall redhead and a bearded hipster.

"I'm Noah, by the way," one of the guys said as the other two moved away with Vivian, his hand outstretched. "Don't mind Viv. She's all heart and no censor."

Rylan shook Noah's hand. "Yeah, I get it. Elena's had quite an impact on everyone here."

"She has. They love her. This promotion is just dotting i's and crossing t's. She's been the boss of games almost from the get-go." Noah rubbed his jaw as he surveyed the spread. "Sabine spares no expense when she's celebrating one of the Cats. Be prepared for a meal like you've never had before."

A last meal. It had that feeling about it…a finality. He didn't like it.

"If you'll excuse me, I need to make a call." He walked to the edge of the deck, scanning the horizon, before pulling his cell out. "Chip, anything I need to know?"

Chip's response was click clacking on his keyboard. "If you're asking if I have a solution to your problem, then the answer is no. These things take time."

"You haven't heard any chatter about us?" There was a hit on Elena that came with a substantial bounty, that was a fact, but it didn't mean anyone planned to take it. "You did say you made sure they know I'm with her?" His reputation preceded him, and he was counting on that to keep the others away until he could get Elena to safety.

"Yeah, I put the word out that you're with her. As far as everyone thinks, you're off the grid. Last known location was New York then your trail went dead."

Chip paused to take a slurpy sip of something. "There are no known takers yet on the bounty. That doesn't mean you're in the clear, but I think anyone sniffing around will only act if they see an opportunity. In other words, don't get sloppy."

"As if." Rylan crossed his arms, his phone still pressed to his ear. "Keep working on a plan. We're heading out of here in a few hours." It was a very small window of opportunity for a hit man or woman to strike. All the same, Rylan wasn't keen on taking any chances. "Don't ignore the rumors. I want to know whatever you hear."

The gossip that ran rampant among the 'murder for hire' community was broken telephone level at the best of times, but Rylan knew there was always some truth to the muddled messages being passed along.

"Will do," Chip said before abruptly hanging up.

Rylan blew out a hard breath, adjusted the lapels on his suit then slid his phone into his pocket. It was going to be a long night but, in the end, he'd have Elena to himself and headed to safety. They'd come up with a plan once he got her secured.

He'd figure out a way to make her happy. Of that, he was certain.

* * * *

Elena had been fighting tears all night. Even with all the laughter and booze, conversation and distractions, she couldn't help the feeling of loss that settled in her stomach and reminded her, with every bite of decadent food, that this was her last meal with her friends.

Cammie sat on her left, Ry on her right. He had his hand on her knee, reassuring her that he was with her in all ways. She was trying to take comfort in that. She'd wanted Ry all to herself for as long as she could remember. She needed to focus on the joy of that.

"It's not like you're going to be on a different planet," Cammie said. "We'll stay in touch."

Elena nodded as the wilted leaves of salad in her mouth turned into rotted mush. She didn't have the heart to tell everyone that she would be disappearing completely. *No keeping in touch. No coming out of hiding.* As much as she loved the idea of being with Ry twenty-four seven, she felt like she was in mourning, grieving the life she could have had...if only her father and stepmother weren't the people they were. If only there was a way to dispose of all the blood money and rid herself of her father's damned legacy once and for all. Changing her name wasn't enough. She'd tried that. Plastic surgery, a new identity, was too ridiculous to consider and yet, Elena felt desperate enough to dwell for a few too many minutes on what a new face could do for her.

"Let's have a toast!" Sabine said as she stood from her spot at the head of the table. "To Elena, our game master extraordinaire. She may be leaving us for sexier pastures"—Sabine winked in Ry's direction, her smile broad, full of hope—"but she will never be forgotten."

Cheers went up around the table. Elena had always been amazed by how Sabine could fake it like a pro. She was the only other person at this table who knew Elena was never coming back and yet she kept the cheer high and the energy pumping. It was like her hope that things would work out was enough to keep the party light.

"And the door is always open, my friend," Sabine added before taking a sip of her drink, reading Elena's mind, as usual.

"Thanks, everyone," Elena said, her voice clogged. She cleared her throat with some wine. "I'm so honored to have worked with all of you." She raised her glass to each of them. "And who knows? Maybe one day I'll be back." Sabine could pretend, so Elena would as well. No sense in bringing everyone else down with her. That was the Kitty Cat way. *Chin up, tits out and smile like someone is watching.*

Ry squeezed her knee.

Everyone clapped, nodded, said nice things about how much they'd miss Elena, their words, their expressions, all nearly toppling over the barricades Elena had built around her emotions. Her heart was full with the love she felt pouring toward her. She would have a damn good cry once she was on the plane, but for now, she was going to enjoy her friends one last time.

"Where are the Jell-O shots?" Elena hollered. "This isn't a proper Cat party without some shooters!"

Another cheer went up and down the table. Sabine waved her hand and servers came with trays of goodies. This was the last Kitty party Elena would attend, so she decided right there and then that she'd make the most out of it.

Ry didn't even give her one of his usual warning side eyes as she snatched two off a passing tray.

"I'll be back in a second. Going to take a call." Ry pushed his seat back, gave her a quick kiss on the forehead then beelined for the other side of the deck.

"Girl time!" Cammie said, already easing out of her chair. "Let's have one last Cat meeting in the restroom."

Elena smiled. While she'd never been one of the escort Kitty Cats, she knew that they often met in lady's washrooms to hash out details of the information they'd gathered through the night. She'd been part of many meetings just by sheer luck over the years but had never been officially invited to one.

She put her napkin on her plate, finished with attempting to force food down. "I'd love that." As she stood, she noted that Viv and Lexi pushed their chairs out as well.

"We're coming!" They both said at the same time.

Elena checked that Ry was still on the phone, hesitating for a second longer than the others. She should tell him where she was going, but his back was to her and she didn't want everyone wondering why she was asking permission to go to the washroom. The restaurant was empty, anyway. Sabine had cleared it out so they'd have the entire place to themselves, and Adam was ever vigilant with security. With a shrug, she turned toward the restaurant, noting that the girls had already disappeared inside.

Elena glanced at the panel of windows with a stunning view of the water, so blue it was purity exemplified. In contrast, two security guys crossed paths, their eyes on the water, binoculars around their thick necks. They gave a darker tone to the beauty of the water and the dangers that might lurk in the distance.

She shivered, dread mingling with her sorrow.

Just as she cleared a second doorway and entered the very empty main dining room, a hand latched onto the back of her arm, making her heart thud all the way up her throat.

Her reflex was to turn and strike, but Ry's voice halted her from doing that. "El, we have to go, *now*."

Ry was still on the phone talking to someone as he steered her around the tables between them and the front door. "You sure it's him?"

She looked over her shoulder at Ry, saw his face and knew there was danger in the area. With one fleeting glance to the outside table where Sabine and the others were chatting, oblivious to what was happening with Ry and Elena, she resolved herself to the reality of her situation. She was going to disappear without getting to say goodbye. While that fact broke her heart, if there was a hitman zeroing in on her, she didn't want him on the hunt for her anywhere near the people she cared about the most.

"Let's go," she said as she took control over where they were going. There was only one door out to the front, and that's where they were headed.

With her heart fluttering, and adrenaline soaking her muscles, she was both jittery and on edge.

Ry said a few muffled words to the security who were on the front door, pausing long enough for them to radio Adam. No one would stop them from leaving. That wasn't the vibe Elena was getting, but they waited to get the all-clear from Adam anyway.

"The plane is ready for takeoff," one of the guys relayed to Ry and Elena. "Adam thinks we should accompany you to the airport."

Ry was already shaking his head, same as Elena.

"No," they both said at the same time.

"Inconspicuous is better. We'll slip out, and take a cab." Ry let go of her arm, his eyes scanning, his body tense. He was still on the phone, listening to someone else talk.

"I don't want anyone here to get hurt," Elena said, hoping Adam would understand.

The security guy nodded once, telling her with zero words that he'd convey her message. He opened the front door, scanned the area, then, once seemingly satisfied, motioned for them to exit.

Ry had his free hand on her arm again, guiding her down the walkway, steady and calm, even though she could tell by the grip on her biceps that he was anything but.

There was another restaurant across the street, music drifting down the road from a bar at the end. Even though Sabine had bought out the seaside restaurant behind them, the rest of the street was packed.

Elena scanned the area thick with tourists. She didn't know what danger looked like, so she saw it in every face that passed them.

"Do you have a location?" Ry said into the phone. "Damn it, Chip. I don't have eyes on anyone here."

A cab headed their way. Elena's heart hammered.

Ry turned away from her, ready to open the door as the cab slid up to the curb.

A hand wrapped around Elena's mouth. And arm snaked over her waist, something pokey pressed between her ribs. "No sudden moves, Miss Russio."

She froze. Ry turned, his eyes widening as he took in the guy holding Elena. She saw the flash of rage spark over his face, his body tensing. The minute flicker of deadly intention gave her a sick sort of reassurance. The guy must have seen it too, because he dug his knife into her side.

She winced, biting her lip to stop any noise from coming out.

"Don't." The guy took a step back, pulling Elena with him. "It's already over, Rylan. You know that," the guy said. "The bounty is too high to pass up."

Something in Ry's eyes said the man spoke the truth. The price on her head was a lot, more than they had originally thought.

"Walk away. Let me have this one." The guy took another step back, easing them into a side street. "You have no obligation to the family now."

Ry mumbled something into the phone, listened, then ended the call. Some kind of resolve flashed over his eyes.

"She can pay you more," Ry said, shocking Elena so she tripped on the next step. The knife dug in deeper, biting against her skin so she knew it'd drawn blood. "Consider the source of that bounty."

"I am." The guy tightened his hold on her, pulling her closer to him, his body pressed against her back. "Someone has to answer for the family's crimes."

"Not her. She's innocent." Ry slipped his phone into his pocket, trailing them as they moved farther into the alley.

"It won't stop until they're all gone. Every single Russio needs to die. You know that."

"Not her," Ry repeated, growling through his words.

Her father put a death sentence on her the second he left her his fortune. That's what this guy was saying.

Elena wouldn't be the one they sacrificed for her father's sins, though. *No fucking way.*

She lifted her foot, slammed her heel straight back into the guy's knee then fell backward as he tried to shift his stance, pushing all her weight into throwing him off balance. The knife slipped into her side, slicing deeper than before, but that didn't stop her from using her weight to change her odds. She stumbled back and back, pushing into him, keeping him off balance and moving him away from the tourists so Ry could do his thing.

Chapter Nineteen

Red fury burned through Rylan as he stalked toward the assassin holding Elena hostage. Rylan knew Kenneth to be as ruthless as he was desperate for money, and by the wild look in his eyes, he was at his most reckless. He wasn't the best of the killers for hire who would be coming, but he wasn't the worst, either.

He also answered to a higher power, and now Rylan knew who was behind the hit, his strategy needed to change.

Elena had Kenneth off balance and on the move, so Rylan followed, taking her lead, watching the knife that still dug into her waist. Blood soaked the green of her dress, sticking to her side, coating the blade.

Her eyes never left his. He felt them burning into his heart, knowing that she was counting on him to get this right, which meant he needed to get his emotions under control or he'd make mistakes that could cost Elena her life.

This was his job. Protect his client. Elena was his client.

She was more than that.

She was his life.

He shook his head like a wild beast, a low growl ripping from his chest. He fought to believe that he could square his feelings for Elena away and stick to business, but there was no controlling the rage inside him. Kenneth had drawn blood. He'd pay for that.

"I'll make it quick. No pain. She gives me the information I need, and it's over." Kenneth was onto her strategy, and he righted himself, dragging Elena up. "Quit making this so hard. She's not your problem anymore, Rylan."

Elena pushed back, trying to hit him with her head. Kenneth dodged, clenched his jaw then latched his hand on her throat. Elena's eyes widened. She gasped. Her hands flew to Kenneth's, digging her nails into his knuckles.

"That's enough!" Rylan roared.

Elena dropped her weight, sliding down so abruptly that Kenneth's grip slipped enough for her to carry herself to the ground, opening up a clean space for Rylan to charge.

He went for the torso, tackling Kenneth back, away from Elena. They rolled along the stones, neither one caring about attracting attention now that the fight was on. Kenneth sliced Rylan along the back, barely getting purchase as Rylan pounded Kenneth's ribs with his fists, hitting hard and fast until he felt the satisfying crunch of bones cracking.

Kenneth moaned then kneed Rylan in the crotch, grazing his balls. It was enough to distract Rylan so Kenneth could get another hit in, this time cracking

Rylan's head back with an open-palm slam to the nose. Blood gushed immediately.

Rylan brought his knees up to push Kenneth away, then he sprang to his feet, blood everywhere as he faced off with the assassin.

"I'm the lesser evil. You know that, Rylan." Kenneth cradled his side as he pushed himself to his feet, staggering a few steps. "The others will torture her. They'll hurt her, bad. You know it. Tell her to give me the information. Make it easy. I promise that the hit will be painless."

"You want me to give her up and what, split the money?" Rylan could barely get the words out. They were so disgusting.

"I'll cut you in, sure, but it won't be fifty-fifty." Kenneth shook his head. "You're a dead man anyway, Rylan. You worked too long for that bastard and his family. It's only a matter of time before there's a hit on you."

"You worked for him, too." Rylan spat blood against the wall.

"Not as long as you did. You were loyal. That's what no one can understand. A man like that? You stayed with him. Says something about you, doesn't it? And now you're with her, protecting her like she's a damn princess. She's not. She's one of them. She was dead the second she was born to that bastard."

Rylan wiped his mouth with his sleeve, his breathing ragged. "I'm loyal, yes, but not to him."

Kenneth's eyes grew wide, he flickered them to Elena, who was sprawled on the ground, clenching her waist. "Ah, I see now." He whacked his head with his hand. "How stupid I've been. Of course, it's her."

"Always for her," Rylan confirmed before he charged Kenneth once again, taking him around the waist and slamming him into the wall.

He drilled Kenneth in the side while taking a hit to the head that had his spine creaking painfully in the wrong direction.

Kenneth laughed, then coughed, blood sputtering from his lips. "A sucker for pussy. That's what's going to get you killed? That's your weak spot?" He punched Rylan in the gut.

They grappled on the ground, kicking dirt up, getting closer to where Elena lay. She kicked at Kenneth, her heels digging into his thigh.

Kenneth grunted, took a swing at Elena's calf, twisting awkwardly to get at her.

Rylan clocked him in the neck, knocking a gasp out of the man, then took his throat, his arm crooked so he could squeeze just by bending his elbow. Kenneth's fight stopped abruptly. He clawed at Rylan's arm, but it was too late. Rylan had a death hold, and he wasn't about to let go.

"I'm not dead yet," Rylan said.

Kenneth went slack. Thirty seconds to knock him out. Two minutes to end his existence. Rylan didn't stop. He couldn't. He'd kill anyone who threatened Elena.

Adrenaline locked his arm. He was frozen in place, cradling Kenneth's lifeless body. "Can you walk? Are you okay? El, tell me, are you hurt?"

"Not much. I'm okay. What do I do?" Her voice was steady...strong. He took comfort in that.

"Get Adam."

"No need." Adam's voice cut the darkness behind them. "We'll take it from here." He tapped Rylan's shoulder, and like a spring release, Ry managed to unlock his arm and let Kenneth go.

The body slid to the ground.

"Sabine would like you both back at the restaurant," Adam said as he nodded to the shadows, "with an escort." Like this was the normal way of things.

Two security guards appeared behind Adam. "Go. I've got this."

Rylan knew the sound of that level of calm. Adam had done this before. He took care of things when they got messy. Elena had not only aligned herself with allies but co-conspirators in dark matters as well. Rylan should have realized that from the start. They had Elena's back—and, by extension, his too.

Elena slipped her arm around his waist, using him as support as they both got up. A small crowd had formed but Adam's guys were dispersing them quickly.

Rylan shifted to check Elena's wounded side, but she waved him away. "It's nothing. I'm fine. Just a scratch." She tightened her grip on his waist, like she was worried she'd lose him.

He squeezed her back, being gentle, while at the same time letting her know he wasn't going anywhere.

His face felt twice its normal size, and his nose throbbed, but having Elena nestled into him was enough to get him walking, following their escorts back to the restaurant. The cat was definitely out of the bag. It was probably time to start asking for the help he now knew Sabine could give.

* * * *

"You two sure know how to make an exit," Sabine said from the edge of the table where she sat watching the medics tend to Elena's flesh wound and his wacked up nose. "You could have told us."

Elena had tears glistening as she winced through the antiseptic spray. "That's not the way Ry works."

"I gathered," Sabine drawled, heavy on the sarcasm.

"It's *my* duty to keep Elena safe," Rylan said, then clenched his jaw as the medic adjusted his nose with a firm crack. Pain splintered up his sinuses, stabbing his brain with fresh agony.

"So, you're her bodyguard. Sent by her notorious father, I assume. How is Cai, anyway? Dead, I'm guessing, if you're here, Rylan."

Elena snapped her head in Sabine's direction, clearly surprised.

"Yes, he died three days ago." Rylan grunted, putting the pieces more firmly together. Sabine knew who Elena was from the get-go if she knew who Cai was.

"Oh fuck, Elena. You didn't really think we had no idea who you were, did you?" Sabine crossed her arms, looking more amused than offended. "I'm the queen of information, darling. I know it all."

"I-I-I didn't want to get you tangled up..." Elena sighed. "I'm sorry. I should have known you were on to me."

"I figured you had your reasons. If my father was Cai Russio, I'd want nothing to do with him, either." Sabine patted her knees then stood. "Now, let's come up with a plan, shall we? The devil knows that these bastards won't stop coming until we do something about it."

"This isn't your fight," Rylan said as he waved away the bandage the medic tried to splint his nose with. The black eyes that were forming would be enough of a signal that he had an exploitable weakness, and he didn't need a bandage to showcase exactly where on his face he was injured. "I'll take Elena to a safe house."

"Like hell you will," Sabine said. "This is our fight now. It's unfolding on our front step. You know word is spreading that she's here. It's only a matter of time before more assassins come. We could fake her death, sure, but I'm not the kind of woman to run and hide — and I don't think Elena is either. If I know her as well as I think I do, she'll want to see this through on her own terms. And frankly, we're better equipped for what you and I both know is coming. You can't do this alone, no matter how good you are."

Rylan opened his mouth to argue, but one look from Elena stopped him cold.

"She's right. I do want to fight. I want to fight for the life I've earned, for the life I deserve. I don't want to pay for Father's crimes with my happiness."

He moved to her, his hands on the sides of her head, his lips against her forehead. "It's going to be dangerous. I can't lose you."

"You won't." She kissed him, her lips soft, plush, tender. "You'd never let anything bad happen to me."

"And neither will I," Sabine added. "You're part of this family, too, El, and we fight for our own."

Rylan nodded as he pulled away. Elena was right. Sabine was right. Better to face the problem head on. He slipped his phone out of his pocket. "I've been working on a plan."

"I hope your plan has room for Adam. He likes a good fight." Sabine laughed. "Things have been quiet lately."

"With all your connections, you wouldn't happen to know Carter Del?" Rylan turned his phone so Sabine could see the screen.

"Can't say I do...yet." Sabine's eyes danced and Rylan couldn't tell if she was excited or intrigued. Both probably. "Is he the one who put a hit on Elena?"

"Who's Carter Del?" Elena asked when Rylan turned his phone for her to look at the screen. Elena scrunched her nose, staring at the photo like she was trying to work something out.

"You don't recognize him, do you?" Rylan zoomed in on the face. "Maybe if you could smell him..."

"Oh my fuck! That's the stable boy from my father's compound!" Elena reeled backward. "He wants to kill me?"

"He's the source of all the hits. Took my intel guy a while to figure it out, but it makes sense now."

"Why would he put a hit on me?" Elena looked genuinely confused. If she only knew the depth of her father's dirty deeds.

"It should have clicked when you told your story about your first kiss." Rylan cursed himself for being so slow.

Elena's hand fluttered to her chest, her mouth open like she was gasping for air.

"I'd forgotten about that kid, but the rumors that started when he showed up were intense." Rylan had only just started working for Cai when the kid came to the compound. "Some of the other guys had said that Carter's entire family had been taken out on Cai's orders, but for some reason, he'd asked that the kid be left alive and brought to him."

"For some reason? My father was a sadistic bastard. He probably loved torturing Carter." Elena's skin paled, and her hand shook. "Is that why he wants me dead?"

"No." Rylan swallowed the lump in his throat. "He wants you dead because he believes your father's fortune rightfully belongs to him."

The puzzle pieces began to click, and realization dawned on Elena's face. "He's related to me, isn't he?" She looked like she was about to vomit. "Please don't tell me I kissed my own brother."

"Allegedly," Rylan said softly. "And only a half-brother."

Elena covered her mouth. "That's so gross!"

"While that is definitely not the kind of revelation I'd be keen on hearing—total *ick*—it is a minor one compared to what you're facing now, darling." Sabine brought the attention back to her. "I need to meet this guy."

"Like I said." Rylan put his phone away. "I have a plan."

"So do I. How do you feel about being bait, sweetie?" Sabine laughed as she pushed herself off the table. "Adam! A word." She continued mumbling to herself as she made her way out of the room. "The nerve, coming after one of my girls! Those goons won't know what hit them."

Chapter Twenty

Ry had made a call, one that Elena knew he didn't want to make. Even though he'd been working on a plan to keep her right where she was, with her newfound friends and family, Elena could tell that he was reluctant to put his plan into action.

She knew why, of course. The plan, like Sabine had suggested, involved Elena playing the role of bait. Not that it was hard to get the hit men moving... She did have a price on her head, and now they knew where to find her.

Carter Del, her, *ick*, half-brother, wanted retribution for her father and stepmother's crimes. She couldn't blame him. Elena understood his anger. She'd lived a luxurious life growing up. She'd wanted for nothing. Her ignorance over what her father had done to give her that life was no excuse. She owed people things... but not with her life. That's where she'd draw a line.

Sabine's plan was an offshoot of Ry's. She'd extended an invitation to the island. Come to listen.

Listening would get the hitmen a little something for themselves, anything beyond that would put them in a world of hurt…and likely death. She'd been very clear on her expectations, and her reputation had, strangely, proceeded her demands. Turns out that assassins also enjoyed Kitty Cat amenities, and Sabine, it seemed, knew this.

Still, it was a tricky balance.

Ry didn't like it. That was clear. He'd rather hunt the assassins down then take them out one by one. Sabine was a negotiator. She knew how to entice men to do her bidding, and she was a powerhouse in her own right. Elena had complete faith.

All the same, Adam and the team were prepared for the worst and so was Ry.

Elena hoped, like every problem that disappeared in her younger life, money would take care of the situation. And frankly, she had it, and Carter did not—which, Elena believed, was the real issue at hand. Money, the solver of most problems, also created just as many. Sabine was moving the pieces to ensure that it was clear to everyone that Carter had no claim on the inheritance. It would never be his. In fact, it was in the process of being completely out of his reach, even if he killed Elena.

All the same, money or not, she armed herself with a knife, complete with a leg holster, one her father had given her when she was a teenager. She'd always carried it with her—in her luggage, her purse—but she didn't ever wear it, not like she was now. The stakes felt different this time. She knew she had to prepare herself to use the weapon. The wound to her side reminded her of that every time she moved.

She wouldn't be facing the assassins. She didn't have a death wish. Sabine would do the talking. Guns would also be turned in if the hitmen wanted on the island. They'd all been made aware of the 'thou shalts' at the moment of invite. Metal detectors, full pat downs, explosive scenting dogs had been brought in from a source on the mainland. They were covered — or at least, Elena hoped they were.

"That's the last of the papers signed," Elena said as she put the heavy pen down, weighted with her decisions and hopes that this would be enough.

Sabine gathered up the documents, shuffling them into a neat pile. "Cammie will get these where they need to be." She came around the desk, the same one that had separated them when Elena had put in her resignation. "This will work. Trust me," Sabine said with a reassuring hug. "You're giving them what they want. They just don't know it yet."

"They want me dead."

"They want payment, and with so many of them in my files, they'll want discretion, too. I've found that money goes a long way to ease demands but so does leverage like I have." She pulled back then tapped her finger to her lips. "And believe me, the kind of information I have will weigh their decisions in our favor."

The fact that Sabine was using the hard-earned intel to save Elena's life wasn't a sacrifice that went unnoticed. Elena knew the significance of what Sabine was doing for her. If she got out of this, Sabine would have her undying loyalty for the rest of her life...no question.

"I want it to do good." The blood money was tainted, but that didn't mean Elena didn't want to use it to help. For a fleeting moment, she thought maybe that money could be used to bolster charities and help the communities that her father had destroyed with his greed. She had a plan for Carter, too, but it depended on whether or not he'd be satisfied with unimaginable wealth in place of revenge. She wasn't sure she'd be able to make that kind of choice and live with it if someone had done to her what their father had done to Carter. She was hoping that he'd see dollar signs and a life of luxury and call off the hit.

They had to take care of the immediate threat first — a bunch of assassins descending on the island — then they'd tackle her half-brother.

"It's doing good. It's saving your life," Sabine said with another reassuring hug. "Don't worry about that side of things. I'll take care of it."

"Showtime, boss," Adam said from the doorway. "Elena, if you'll go with Ben, he'll make sure you're protected."

She wanted to ask where Ry was, but she knew he was in the thick of their plan. He might not be guarding her, at her side, like she wanted, but he wasn't abandoning her, either. She had to trust this process. She rubbed her hand over the lump of her skirt where the knife was resting against her thigh. All it would take was a flick of her thumb and a tug, then the knife would slide down and be ready for use in an instant.

She hoped she didn't have to use it.

She had to trust that if it came down to it, she'd protect herself just as she'd always done.

They rounded a corner toward Sabine's wing of the resort when Ry stepped out of a door to her left like he knew she'd be there. He was wearing a black suit, complete with a black matte button-up shirt. He looked like a grim reaper, his standard uniform in times like these. She knew he had weapons concealed all over his body, but it was his body alone that was the deadliest weapon. She'd seen him in action too many times not to take comfort in that.

"El," Ry said, his voice hoarse.

"Meet me at the end of the hall when you're done," Ben said as he nodded at Ry then continued walking.

Ry nodded back, then wasted no time in pulling Elena into his arms. She tilted her face up and fought not to cry. His expression was so serious, dire really, and that scared her more than anything else.

"Don't do anything reckless, Ry," Elena said, an echo of words he'd used with her many times over their on-again, off-again lives together.

Ry chuckled softly. "You would say that." His expression flickered dangerously close to grief, and Elena's heart twisted. He thought this was the last time he would see her. Deep down she knew he'd sacrifice everything, even himself, to save her life.

"Ry, there is no me without you." She moved up his body, her hands in his hair, pulling his head down so she could kiss him with her heart and her fear and her hope. When she pulled back, she pressed her head into the crook of his neck, standing on tiptoe to accomplish that. "Please be careful. I need you."

Ry slipped his fingers under her chin then tilted her head up so he could meet her eyes. "El, you're an amazing woman, and you can do anything, even live without me."

His words had a finality to them that made tears slip from her eyes, despite her effort to hold them back.

"Ry—"

He didn't let her speak. Instead, he kissed her with everything he had, and she felt his love, his passion and his hope.

He would do everything he could to come back to her. That was what his kiss said.

Chapter Twenty-One

The rest of the Cats had been given the option to leave or play. They'd sent their partners home, and each and every one of them had decided to stay. That level of devotion to Sabine and to Elena, had blown Rylan's mind. Adam, and team, had stayed behind, of course, but so had Missy the sheriff, and Zane and Cammie, Lexi and Sam and Vivian and her trio of men.

Sabine hadn't just invited the assassins for a chat. She'd invited them for the gentlemen's club experience, which meant her Cats would be working the room to glean the information they needed. As soon as they found out where Carter was, he'd go take care of the problem for good.

Elena had graciously granted Carter a choice. Ry would have no problem erasing him from the earth if he didn't choose the right option.

In a matter of half a day, Sabine and her team had pulled together a party that rivaled any New York Christmas bash Rylan had ever heard of. The main dining hall had been converted to a disco lounge, chairs that were double-wide and perfect for couples to sit on, along with tables, chairs, pool tables and poker games ready to go. There was food, buffet-style along one wall, complete with a chocolate fountain and enough booze flowing to drown a person — or at least soak them so heavy that they'd agree to just about anything. Sabine had laid down a wonderland of vices for the men she'd invited, men who Rylan knew would fall for the lure of attending something connected to a Kitty Cat Club experience.

The hitmen were under no delusion. In order to be allowed in, they had to give up all weapons, not that it mattered to men like these. They could make a weapon out of just about anything, but at least the security team didn't have to worry as much about guns and machetes or any other concealed blade or explosive the assassins might have on them.

Chip had narrowed down the list to ten assassins who had taken the ticket to hit Elena, minus Kenneth, who was no longer on the job. There was a system, of course, for these things, which ensured accountability in a fucked-up way. Ten tickets in total kept the pool small, so if more than one assassin got the hit, which sometimes happened, they'd be splitting the fee in a satisfying way. More than one split would make the bounty not worth the effort. If an assassin was taken out, then a ticket became available. But tonight was about putting a stop to that possibility by finding out where the source of the hit was hiding then ending him and the bounty at the same time. *Two birds, one stone.*

Elena's life was worth two million dollars. That's what the bounty would pay.

Elena was putting up half the money for each assassin, a signing bonus to walk away rather than take their chances with her team of guards. Sabine had full confidence that after wining and dining the hardened mercenaries, they'd give her what she wanted — information — and take the deal. Rylan hoped she was right, but just in case she wasn't, he was ready to fight for Elena's life.

Sabine said he wouldn't have to. She had an ace to play that she assured him would put an end to each and every one of the assassins thirsting for Elena's blood.

"Who's ready to party?" Sonia called out, rousing a cheer from the Cats who were all streaming into the room, decked out in sparkly dresses with low plunging necklines and slits up their thighs. They were smiling, holding bottles of champagne and flutes, moving around the room in stiletto heels that looked like death traps on stilts — and doing it with ease.

They all seemed to be positioning themselves, winks and hand motions passing messages to one another that meant something Rylan couldn't quite figure out. What he did know was that these women were professionals, and they absolutely knew what they were doing. Despite the danger, these Cats were no cowards, and for that he had a lot of respect.

Sabine wasn't running an escort agency as much as she was running a team of spies, and they all knew how to do their jobs like pros. He was in awe watching them greet the hitmen as the men stepped into the room, adjusting their clothes like they'd just got frisked within an inch of their lives, which they had. Irritated expressions quickly changed to delight and intrigue as the Cats sidled up to them, some taking on two men and coaxing them away from the door and into the shadows of the grand room. *Distraction at its best.*

Rylan was itching to do something, to use violence to get the truth out of these guys. But he knew them all in one way or another, which meant he knew how impossible it would be to get them to talk with anything but finesse — the kind of finesse these women had.

Rylan stood alert, watching from the sidelines, trying to be as inconspicuous as possible.

Some of the men were warier than others, waving away the attention of the Cats, sitting rigid, their backs to the walls, scanning the room for traps. Others, the more reckless of the bunch, were fully engaged with the offerings…slamming shots and stuffing food down their throats.

"Not sure how you're going to get those guys to talk," Rylan said to Adam, who had sidled up next to him in the shadows. He motioned to the spattering of men who were standoffish.

"Oh, we have our ways." Adam nodded up to the rafters. "We pump lavender, vanilla and lemongrass into the rooms for situations like this. Calms the beasts."

Rylan turned his head to take in Adam's profile. "And how many situations like this do you have usually?"

By Adam's answering smirk, Rylan would guess a lot.

"Right, so we wait for the incense infusion to take effect…then we pounce." He couldn't keep the sarcasm from slipping out.

"We wait for the scents to set the mood." Adam patted his arm on his way to the door. "Then we let the Cats really do their thing. But first, Sabine will have her way."

"Welcome, gentlemen!" Sabine's voice boomed over the music, her mic turned on full blast, capturing the attention of every assassin in attendance. The music was lowered to a whisper so that Sabine's next words came through loud and clear. "You've come tonight to hear a proposal."

"We're here tonight to get some action!" one of the guys in the back yelled.

"If you're a good boy," Sabine said with a sly wink, "maybe you'll see some action."

"Ain't no good boys here, lady," someone else shouted.

The men all laughed.

So did the Cats and so did Sabine...but her laugh turned sharp, cutting, and dulled the buzz significantly. She lost her smile, narrowed her eyes, and seemed to grow ten feet as she stared out into the crowd. Rylan got a chill. She was commanding and a little terrifying. He couldn't say why, but the effect it had on the room was abrupt. Only a few men chuckled awkwardly as she stood waiting for silence.

Once the room had quieted and all eyes were on her again, she began.

"As you know, I'm a businesswoman with a primary goal of satiating needs, wants and desires." She paused as if waiting for a lewd comment. The assassins had seemingly learned, and no one so much as coughed. "And tonight, you're here to achieve those three things."

She motioned for the Cats to move, and they did, each carrying an iPad to the men.

"As you will see, the funds that your employer is after are not ever going to be available to him." She waited while the Cats showed screens to the men, giving them access to swipe and read, their eyes scanning transaction reports and banking statements. "Cai Russio left his entire fortune to his daughter with no provisions for an illegitimate, unprovable son. Which means" — she waited a beat for the Cats to show another screen — "that your bounty can't be paid by Carter because he's broke. The only way he can pay the bounty is if he gets Elena to transfer the funds to him before he kills her. And now, as you see, that can never happen. The funds are locked in a trust with very specific guidelines on how it can be used. You'll also see the provisions that have been made in each of your names or aliases." She waved her hand. "I'll give you all a few moments to study the information we've given you."

There was a low murmur of sound as the men began to consult with one another. It was an unusual sight. Rylan didn't think he'd ever see the day that assassins would work together on anything, let alone have a meeting to discuss a plan forward that didn't involve killing.

"One more thing," Sabine said, her voice projecting above the din of conversation. Quiet settled over the crowd. "This is an all-or-nothing deal. You want the guaranteed payout? Then you all have to agree to take it, which means you all have to sign a contract with me that ensures Elena's safety. You'll be her protectors, not her hunters. You will do anything to ensure she lives, because if you don't, the money stops flowing. If you don't, you'll have to answer to me." She leaned forward, seemingly making unflinching eye contact with each of the men. "Each of you has a reason to stay on my good side."

The Cats each swiped the screens of their iPads then moved the devices back into the hitmen's line of sight.

"And, with that, a promise of pain that you don't want to test," Sabine said, her tone brokering no nonsense.

The woman had just threatened a room full of assassins. Rylan had to fight to keep his mouth from gaping, his body tensed, expecting immediate backlash. He scanned the group, and what he saw was a testament to her persuasion.

Their expressions said, take the path of least resistance.

Their expressions said, probably better not to fuck with this woman.

Their expressions said they wanted the payout.

Chapter Twenty-Two

Elena wasn't usually a sit-around-and-wait kind of person but the situation as it was demanded she be one now. And that...well, it sucked. She was feeling claustrophobic, even though the room she was in had floor-to-ceiling windows overlooking the lush forest behind the compound. And it was by no means a small room. An office of sorts, the room Elena was killing time in had a desk built into one wall and two plush couches kitty-corner to one another with a large, upholstered ottoman in the center. She'd tried to relax on the couch. She'd attempted to distract herself by reading one of the many magazines strewn around the room. She'd even, for a few moments, tried losing herself in the financial statements that Sabine had sent to her outlining the future of her father's blood money.

None of that had worked. She was worried, for herself, yes, but more so for Ry. On the other side of the compound, nine assassins indulged in Kitty Cat festivities. Nine skilled killers who had come to get

Elena. And Ry would do anything to stop them from getting to her.

He was good—Elena knew from experience—but could he take on nine of them?

Yes, he wasn't alone. Adam and his team would back Ry up, no matter what happened, but did any of them really know how this could go?

The answer to both questions was a big fat no, and that had Elena's anxiety spiking so hard that she could sit still.

"Ugh!" She paced another circuit around the room, rubbing her hands together like that would ease her stress.

She needed a punching bag…or a treadmill. Maybe working out her frustration in a physical way would distract her from what was going on in the banquet room.

Ben was just outside the door. He'd offered her food service an hour before, but she'd declined. Her stomach had been in knots and in no mood for sustenance.

But maybe she should have a tea, something to calm her down.

She beelined to the door, but before she could turn the knob, it opened like it sensed her approach.

"Oh, hi," Elena said, taken back by the sudden appearance of Sonia, who was dressed in her usual stunning on-duty Cat apparel, a pair of skintight black sequined short shorts and pink tank. With her large breasts, slim waist and high ponytail, they'd all nicknamed her Lara Croft after the video game character that many men found droolworthy. "How's it going out there?"

Sonia wasn't smiling and Elena took that to be a bad sign. Her stomach dropped to her toes. "Oh no, what's happened? Is Ry okay?"

"He's fine," Sonia said as she turned the lock behind her.

"I don't believe you. Tell me what's going on." Elena started for the door again.

Sonia stepped in front of her, then, without warning, she elbowed Elena in the face. The pain was immediate and shocking. Her nose exploded, bright lights danced across her vision, she staggered back and blood shot in a spray that landed across Sonia's chest.

All Elena could do was lift her arms to ward off another blow, but Sonia used her surprise attack momentum to knock Elena onto the couch so she sprawled precariously off balance, one hand on the floor to keep herself from rolling off, blood dripping down her chin.

"Stay there," Sonia ordered, "or I'll hit you again."

She disappeared for a few seconds then returned to Elena, who was still processing what had just happened. Her head was on fire, beating to a frantic tune that pummeled her brain. She'd never been hit before—not like that—and she couldn't think beyond one word, *Sonia?*

"Oh, honey," Sonia said in a mockingly sweet voice. "Here… Use this to stop the bleeding." She pushed a wad of tissue at Elena's face, crushing her already throbbing nose with too much pressure.

"Ow!" Elena tried to right herself, but the way she was leaning, half on the couch, half off, gave Sonia an advantage. Fresh pain shot up her nose, stabbing her in the brain like a hot poker as Sonia pressed harder on the tissue. "Stop!"

Sonia pulled herself back, her face twisted in a dangerous smirk. "Anything for you, El. Here… Let me help." She forced Elena sit up, moving her roughly into an awkward upright position. The tissue fell to Elena's lap at the same time that Sonia yanked her wrists behind her back, twisting suddenly so new pain radiated up her arm. "Pressure points, sweetheart. You should learn how to use them."

Her arms felt numb, her wrist throbbed, her brain was full of chaos and Sonia tied her up with something strong, unyielding and tight.

"There," Sonia sighed as she sat down on the ottoman then crossed her legs. "All settled."

Elena tested the limits of the binding. There was no wiggle room.

"Too bad you sucked so hard at getting out of the ropes yesterday, eh? If you'd been paying more attention, I might be worried about you escaping. But as it is..." She shrugged. "I'm pretty confident you'll stay where I put you."

"What's going on?" Elena, a mile behind the eight ball, still couldn't sort out why Sonia was doing this.

She fought to clear her thoughts, to ignore the pain, but every breath she took burned like lava. Ben... He was outside the door probably thinking that Sonia was here to keep her friend company. The realization had her opening her mouth to shout his name, but Sonia was on her in a second, pressing her knee into Elena's belly, squeezing her hands into Elena's neck.

"Don't you dare," Sonia growled. "I don't need you conscious to get what I want."

Elena struggled for a breath, but Sonia had her air completely cut off. She stared into her best friend's cold eyes and wondered if she'd always been this duplicitous. She was in a dangerous situation, but she didn't know what kind of danger yet.

"You're fading, friend," Sonia said as Elena's eyelids drooped and her thoughts scattered. "You gonna behave?"

Elena managed a slight nod.

"Excellent." Sonia grinned and let Elena go.

Sucking in fresh air actually burned Elena's throat but she drank it in quickly.

Sonia settled back on the ottoman, her hands folded on her knees like they were about to have a casual chat. "A few years ago, right around the time you came to join the Cats, I was approached by one of my newer clients, Carter."

Carter my half-brother?

"And he offered to pay me to keep an eye on you."

Each time she filled her lungs brought clarity.

Carter knew where I was the whole time? Who I was? Carter was a client? Fuck.

"I was intrigued, of course. Who is this Elena Sasser? He paid me to get close to you. He said you were from a very important family and that your family owed him something."

She raised her hand as if Elena interrupted her.

"I didn't know your true identity until recently. When we came to the island, actually... Carter let me in on more details. Your father was a very bad man, El." She shook her head. "I mean, no wonder you ran away and changed your name. I don't blame you one bit."

"I'm not like my father," Elena croaked, her throat still raw and sore.

"Well, we both know how cutthroat you can be when you want something." She waved her hand like she was dismissing Elena. "I mean, you kicked my ass all over the place when it came to getting Sabine's attention."

"Sonia, you're my friend. I'd never do anything to hurt you."

"That's debatable," Sonia said. "You certainly didn't let me get in the way of your goals. You'd barrel right over anyone who got in your way."

"And for that you punch me in the face?" Elena fought tears, not because of the pain from her probably broken nose but because she really had trusted Sonia. "And you're wrong. I did help you. I made sure you got the credit that was due to you." But that wasn't the point. She realized now that Sonia was taking her jealousy out on Elena and had misplaced her trust in Carter. "What you're doing right now? It's serious. It's my life, Sonia. Are you saying you want me dead? Because Carter does. He wants me gone."

"Oh God no!" Sonia's cheeks turned pink, like she was scandalized. "Please, El, don't be so stupid. This is nothing personal at all. I know it might seem like it is, but I'm seriously not that petty." She huffed like she was the one who's been offended. "I do still like you, mostly, I mean, you've got that whole Sabine kiss-ass vibe about you all the time, but for what it's worth, I do consider you a friend. Not a BFF or anything... Like, I wouldn't throw myself in front of a bullet for you, and well, Carter made me a really rich woman, and now that source of income is over because he's broke. I need a cash infusion to keep my lifestyle where I want it to be and my future secure."

She was rambling, as if Elena cared about her excuses. The betrayal alone made Elena's head too full of WTFs.

"Especially since, after this, I'm going to have to disappear. And, as you know, Carter needs the money he believes he's owed." She raised her hand as if to stop Elena from arguing, but Elena had no words...none. This was all too bizarre. "I know... I know... Whether or not he deserves your father's money is debatable. He did try to have the man killed many times over, but still, I'm in a situation where two birds, one stone will work to my benefit. So…" She leaned closer like they were co-conspirators. "Why don't you hand over all the banking information Carter will need to get his hands on your inheritance, and we'll call it a day. I'll leave you here, tied up, of course, waiting for your hero to save you, get Carter what he wants and he's promised that he'll call off the assassins. Good deal, right? With one assassin down, a replacement is on the way. That's what Carter said, and that means that Sabine's plan to seduce the men out there won't work on the new hitman, especially because it's a woman. This is the best plan. You don't need money. Sabine loves you! All that ass-kissing has definitely paid off. She'll make you rich. And you have the love of your life finally with you, so really, you've already won the jackpot." She sucked in a sharp breath then let it out with a grin. "It's a win, win!" She grabbed Elena's phone from the floor where it had dropped. "What's your passcode for the bank?"

Elena stared dumbly at the phone, because Sonia truly couldn't be that stupid, could she?

"Oh, come on. I wasn't going to actually knock you out with the whole strangling thing. I just needed you to pay attention."

"There's no money." Elena's tongue felt thick, and the words came out slowly, not because of her burning throat but because she couldn't believe this was Sonia's grand plan.

Sonia rolled her eyes then leaned, holding the phone up to Elena's face so the face recognition would work. "Carter says there's millions."

"Millions, yes, but I can't touch any of it now." Elena's brain began to realign, her thoughts snapping to cohesiveness again, the fog of pain and hurt of

Sonia's betrayal shifting to the background. "Sabine set up trusts—"

"Yes, yes, I know but Carter says there's a way to reverse it." Sonia was frowning at Elena's phone.

"Then Carter's an idiot." Elena wiggled her arms, moving her wrists against the pressure of the rope. She'd gone through many training sessions on escaping restraints, but none of the practices had involved the amount of adrenaline she had coursing through her body. "I signed the management of the funds away to a lawyer. It's gone... I'm giving it all away."

"Of course you are." Sonia rubbed her hand over her face. "Seriously, Elena, do you have any sense of self-preservation?" She shook her head. "All you had to do was keep the money for yourself, gracefully accept that you're a gazillionaire then there wouldn't be a problem right now. You'd be able to give all the money to your stepbrother. Instead, you do whatever Sabine tells you to do, as usual."

"You don't understand. That money is tainted. I don't want it."

"So self-righteous!" Sonia stood abruptly. "I'm going to have to call Carter. Figure out what to do."

"Sonia, you don't have to do this. I can match whatever he said he'd pay you." The words tasted like poison coming out of her mouth because really, she wanted to kick Sonia in the teeth for her betrayal, but unlike what her former friend thought, Elena did have a sense of self-preservation.

"We both know that's a lie." Sonia slipped her phone out from her halter top strap. "You just said you gave it all away. That the money is gone."

"Carter?" Sonia turned her back to Elena. "Yeah, we have a problem."

Elena tried to clear her thoughts of panic and focus on the rope around her wrists. More specifically, she concentrated on the knot and how it looped over and around. She stretched her fingers to find the ends, racking her brain to remember what gestures Ry had used when he was guiding Sonia through untying herself on the adventure tour. She would have used one of those knots for sure.

Pull this side? Tug the loop? All her training was falling apart. All her self-defense techniques were gone from her mind. Panic was taking over. As soon as Carter realized there was no money, he'd tell Sonia to kill her. Would her former friend be able to? That, Elena didn't know.

Sweat broke across her forehead and dampened the back of her neck. Her face throbbed to the beat of her heart, and her stomach was a tight stone weighing her down.

Think. Think.

Pull this piece… She felt a little give. Twist this way. Another tiny bit of room. A surge of hope flushed through her, warm against the panic she felt.

She rotated her wrists and pulled, but the knot held firm.

Fuck.

"Okay, Carter, you're on speaker." Sonia turned with the phone flat in her hand, looking expectedly at it.

"Elena, you know the situation. You know how important it is for your future to give me the money I'm owed." It was strange hearing his voice. It was the same voice of the teen boy she remembered, maybe more mature, thicker, but not very changed from back then and that kind of fucked with her head, because she could only picture him as a teenager, harmless and shy.

"Now, I know you're not a stupid woman. I know you wouldn't lock up all the money, now knowing that I'll have you killed if I don't get my inheritance." Underneath his threat was a hint of desperation.

"You were going to have me killed, no matter what." Elena's laugh was bitter and hard. "You put a price on my head, Carter. That doesn't exactly inspire me to want to help you."

Sonia snapped her eyes up from the phone, a knowing grin suddenly on her face. "See? I told you she was lying. She obviously has money squirreled away. Tell him how to get the money, El, and this will all be over."

Elena had money. Not millions but she had a bank account. She had savings. She could fool him long enough to get herself out of this mess.

"What assurances do I have that you won't betray me?" Elena stabbed Sonia with a hate-filled sneer. "It seems as though I can't trust my friends, and we both know that our family connection is tentative." Elena continued tugging at the rope. There had to be a way to get free.

Sonia's expression crumbled like she was truly hurt by Elena's words.

"Now, don't be like that, sis." Carter sighed. "I have fond memories of you—and not just because of your little crush back in the day." He laughed. Elena cringed, bile rising to the back of her throat. "I swear I didn't know that we were related back then. Didn't find out until much later, after he'd used me then sent me away like a stray dog. I know you aren't like Cai. You're loyal and kind, compassionate. Sonia has been a true friend to you, even if you don't see it. She's softened me toward you over the years. You truly are a remarkable woman, so don't take it out on Sonia. She's just doing what's best for her, very much like you have been doing over the years."

Elena snorted to cover up a grunt of pain, her fingers twisting at an impossible angle to drag the farthest end of the rope down. With a yank, she was free, the rope falling away. It was shocking and sudden. Triumph blasted through her, but somehow she kept her face stoic. "A friend wouldn't do what Sonia is doing."

"Let's just get down to business then," Carter snapped. "Give me the details I need. You have my word, for whatever that's worth, that I won't harm you."

Elena took a moment, pretending she was debating.

"I have your word? You'll call the hit off?"

Sonia nodded.

"On my life," Carter said.

"My bank is Sunset Financial, username Elena Sasser@cowanenterprises.com." Elena rubbed her wrists to get the feeling back. "Password is eight, four, two, nine, nine one."

Sonia smiled a pure shit-eating grin.

Carter mumbled something. The clacking of his typing echoing from the phone. "What the fuck is this—?"

Elena leapt up, an otherworldly scream gushing from her mouth like a torrent of fury. She grabbed the knife from her leg sheath then dove at Sonia, tackling her around the waist and taking her down in a heap of arms, legs, gasps of shock.

Ben charged into the room, calling for backup.

Elena kept her weight pressed into Sonia, her knife firmly against her ex-friend's throat. "If you move an inch, I'll make you bleed."

Sonia had tears already streaming out of her wide eyes, snot already bubbling. "Please, please, I didn't mean it. I wouldn't have let anyone hurt you, El. You *have* to believe me."

Ben helped Elena up as two more guards came in. "Secure her." Ben eased the knife out of Elena's tight grip.

Carter's voice was a wobbly echo from the phone, shouting obscenities. Elena pulled away from Ben to pick it up.

"You're a dead woman, Elena!" Carter screamed. "This account is pitiful. A few thousand isn't what I'm owed! Where's my money!"

"What you have there is my personal account. *My* hard-earned money." Elena switched over from speaker phone. "You're welcome to it, not that I think it'll do you any good."

"I'm going to kill you, bitch!"

"Not if I kill you first." Elena ended the call then dropped the phone from her shaking fingers.

Chapter Twenty-Three

They didn't speak about what happened.

It wasn't that Rylan didn't want to admit to the brutality of his work, but when it came to Elena, it was complicated.

He'd approached Carter with a choice, and the man had answered him with a bullet shot from an antique pocket gun.

Rylan's throat had been grazed, enough to leave a scar that Elena would fret over for the rest of their lives but not enough to slow him down.

"The payments are flowing," Sabine said as a rounding out of their business discussion. "All of Cai Russio's money is divided and distributed, just as Elena wants."

She'd invested all that she had. The money that wasn't being used to pay the assassins was being funneled to charities. The cash infusions would go a long way, Rylan was sure, and the method Sabine's accountant had invested it all would mean it would last an eternity.

He knew that would make Elena happy and relieve her of the guilt she always carried over her family's horrific past.

"That's not why I'm here, but thanks for letting me know." Rylan had requested the private meeting to discuss a few things and to get her help. Elena didn't know he'd returned yet, and she'd probably kill him if she found out that his first stop had been to see her boss and not her.

Sabine quirked an eyebrow. She was seated behind a glass desk, her legs crossed at the knee and elbows on the top, leaning forward like she was riveted to whatever would come out of his mouth next.

"I have a little bit of money." He had a lot of money. He hadn't been working for the Russio clan for free all those years. With his other expenses always taken care of—housing, food, travel—he'd had very little reason to spend anything he'd earned. "And I'd like your help investing it in both mine and Elena's names."

"Both your names?"

"In case something happens to me, I want her to have access to it."

"And how much are we talking about?"

"Five point five, give or take."

"Wow, okay. I can set something up. I'll give my accountant a call."

"Great, thanks." He hesitated before speaking again.

"That's not the only reason you're here, though, right? I mean, by the expression on your face, I feel like there's more coming. A bigger ask." Sabine was frowning, like she expected something bad.

"I've spent my whole adult life living for other people, doing what they wanted me to do." This was hard to say out loud to a virtual stranger, but there was something about Sabine that Rylan instinctively trusted. "I want to... Well...I'm not sure what I want to do, but I know I want to do something for El... something big. To show her...you know...how much I—"

"Love her?" Sabine let out a sharp breath that almost sounded like a *squee* and pushed herself back in her chair. "Well, I can definitely help with that." She pretended to wipe her brow as if he'd made her sweat. "For a second there, I had a fear that you were trying to cut and run."

"Cut and run?" Dread pooled in his gut as he realized what Sabine must think of him and that she was right to suspect he might look for a way out after reporting in having taken care of Carter. "Nah, Elena's stuck with me now. I just want to make up for the years I was a stubborn idiot."

"Not stubborn and not an idiot...not much anyway. You were acting on your principles. Nothing wrong with that. You were just a bit dogmatic about it."

He couldn't argue. Dogmatic was a nicer way of saying that he'd been a stubborn ass about it. "Can you help me?"

"Of course I can. What you want is a grand gesture, and I've got a team of people who are experts in coming up with the perfect kind of grand gesture for any occasion."

"Even the 'forgive-me-for-wasting-years-that-we-could-have-been-together' occasion?"

"Yes, even that." She scrolled through her phone. "Leave it with me. Someone from the team will reach out and get things rolling, planning-wise."

Rylan felt a weight lift. "Elena in the building somewhere?" He pushed himself from the chair.

"Of course," Sabine said as she glanced up from her phone. "She was back at work the day after we got home."

"Where do I find her?"

By the smile on Sabine's face, Rylan knew he was in for it.

"She's running a training session for some Cats...second floor, left off the elevator."

"Room number?"

"Oh...you'll find her. Just listen for the giggles."

Listen for the giggles. "Got it."

"And Rylan?"

He turned back to Sabine.

Her eyes were still glued to her phone as she said, "Tell Elena that she has the rest of the day off."

He grinned as he headed to the door. "Will do."

Chapter Twenty-Four

Elena had been doing her best to distract herself from Rylan's absence. Even though she'd spent most of her adult life without him, she was having a hard time stepping back into the mindset that she could live without him. She knew she could... It was more that she didn't want to.

He'd already told her over the phone that he was coming to New York. She just didn't know if he meant for good or for closure. She hoped it was for good. She wanted it to be. But she knew how Ry got with the dark side of his life, and even though he hadn't confirmed, she also knew that he'd killed her half-brother. He had to, because there was no way Carter would let her live in peace.

As much as she didn't know how to deal with that, she also *did* know that Ry would do anything to keep her safe, and she'd accepted a long time ago that keeping her safe often meant someone had to die. That wasn't her fault. She was a victim of her father's shitty ways.

Or, at least, that's what her therapist told her. Elena was still trying to accept a new way of thinking. She mourned the loss of a brother she hadn't known she had and the life he'd been forced to live — the details of which she could only imagine were horrible, because her father had been a petty, punishing man.

But that deep thinking was something she learned to compartmentalize. She'd deal with those feelings later. Right now she was having a good time.

She was running drills with the Cats, taking them through some adventure tour scenarios and working on what to do with the downtime. Sabine had loved that she'd paid attention to what the losers would have to do while waiting to move on to the next challenge.

"That's exactly what we need to do, Kasey! Cats, take a look at what's going on here." Elena's voice was a whisper compared to the laughing and giggly talk of the Cats in attendance. They were all having a great time, which is how Elena wanted her training sessions to go. "Cats! Over here for a second!" She raised her voice higher, projecting across the open-concept training room. "Kasey isn't going to keep her ass up like this forever!"

More laughter echoed around her, along with catcalls and hoots. Elena felt the air shift against her back, and she didn't have to turn to know someone had walked into the room.

"Now that's not something you see every day." Ry's voice washed over her like a balm to her soul.

She spun directly into his arms. "You're back!" She heaved herself up on tiptoes and kissed him quickly, taking him by surprise as he wrapped his arms around her. "Oh, my fuck, you're hurt." She zeroed in on the wound to his throat, knowing instantly that whatever had happened had been self-defense.

He stopped her from touching the stitches. "I'm good. Just a scratch."

"A scratch!" She examined the two-inch wound. It looked deep. It looked like it could have been a close one. It looked like confirmation that her brother had made the wrong choice. "Any deeper and that would have killed you."

"I'm still here."

"For how long?" She held her breath, hoping, always hoping that he'd tell her what she wanted to hear.

He looked over the top of her head and she knew by his expression that they had an audience. "Is there somewhere we can talk...privately?"

Her gut bottomed out and she slipped herself out of his arms. *No grand gestures here.* "Of course, yeah." She turned to face the crowd of Cats, battling a frown and the tearing of her heart. "Hey, ladies, keep practicing, keep innovating. I'll be back in a bit."

"Sabine says you have the rest of the day off." Ry said the words like a command.

Why? She wanted to ask. *Because he's about to shatter my heart for good?*

She didn't have words, so instead of saying anything, she gestured to the hall. He swept her up, pulling her into his side and nuzzling her throat. "I was thinking somewhere more private."

This didn't feel like bad news. Her heart thundered. She put her hand on his chest to stop him from taking another step.

"Tell me." She fought to look at him, to see his expression and know what his intentions were. "Are you staying or going?"

His eyes widened like her question was the furthest thing on his mind. He pulled her into him, hauling her up his body, lowering his head and kissing her so deeply that her mind cleared of any doubt, any thought, really, and her toes curled, her heart soared and her breath stuck.

"I'm not going anywhere," he said as he tore his lips away. "Now, let's go someplace private."

He picked her up, cradling her in his arms as he nuzzled her throat, clearly waiting for her to direct him. Because he meant somewhere private here... Because he couldn't wait to get her alone... Because he was hers. *Finally.*

"Over there...down the hall...thir—" She moaned as he nibbled her ear. "Third door on the left."

Despite continuing to torture her with his lips, he got them to her office before she could really sense that they were moving. She was so distracted by the reality of what was happening and how surreal it felt to have Ry with her, part of her life, taking her to her office to ravish her.

This was a fantasy she'd had many times — different locations, various set-ups but always Ry, sweeping her off her feet and finally agreeing to what had always been true... They belonged together. They were meant for each other. He was and would forever be, part of her soul.

He kicked her door open, somehow not busting it right off the hinges, then kicked it closed behind them.

Her new office gave her fizzies as it was — pride, joy, a sense of accomplishment, it all buzzed through her every time she walked into the space—but Ry carrying her over the threshold felt like a christening that was about to make things serious.

Seriously hot, that is.

He let her slide down his body, dropping her legs gently while holding her arms, forcing her to meet his intense gaze, his eyes hooded, lips parted, breathing deep like he was sucking her into his soul.

"I will spend the rest of my life convincing you that I'm here, with you, forever."

Elena beamed, her heart filling up with so much joy it felt ready to burst out of her mouth.

"I'd like that," she said, her voice sounding unexpectedly coy. It was hard to believe that this wasn't a dream. "I'd *really* like that."

"But words are nothing without action." He didn't wait for her to react to his words. Instead, he cupped her ass and lifted her so she was eye level, her legs instinctively wrapping around his waist.

His body was hard against hers, honed in ways she could never understand but appreciated all the same. She laid her hands on his cheeks, holding him in place so she could take in his expression, see his eyes, know for certain that he was there with her, in this together, no hesitation.

"I've waited a long time for this." She needed him to understand how much she loved him, needed him, wanted him.

"And we have all afternoon to do it right," Ry said.

She giggled, threw her head back, shivered with tremors when he kissed her throat and nibbled her jaw. He walked them to the couch, plush leather and ready for her body to sink into.

He followed her down to his knees, easing her ass onto the cushions, then pulled her legs from his waist, keeping them open so her heat, her want, was right there in his face.

"I want to hear all the noises you make, El." He pushed her athletic skirt up only to realize that it was built with shorts attached. "What the fuck are these?"

"It's a skort." His expression was too comical not to laugh. "Essential training outfit."

"A skort." He shook his head as he fingered the hem at her thigh. "Not as easy access as a skirt."

Noted. "The prize is worth the trouble."

"Oh, I know it is." He lifted her ass with one hand then peeled her skort off with the other. One fluid motion, with no effort at all, a few tugs and her bottoms were across the room in a heap, a testament to how little Ry cared for the skort barrier.

Gosh, she loved teasing him. When his focus landed on her panties, he sucked in a sharp breath. They were white, lacy and did very little to cover her pussy with a red ribbon thong that trailed up her ass.

"Who did you wear these for?" He fingered the delicate material, tickling her hip.

"Everything I wear is for you, Ry."

"Did you know I was coming today?"

"No." She cleared her throat, being vulnerable was hard. "I dress for you every day, Ry, always have. You're the only man for me. I told you that. I buy the things I love but I wear them hoping that you'll see them."

He grew quiet, lowered his eyes, bit his lip. "I've wasted so much time."

She nudged his chin with her fingers, forcing him to look at her again. "So don't waste any more, okay?"

He rubbed his thumb along her pelvis, coaxing her to open her legs wider as he traced a shivery trail along the creases of her crotch, where her panties gripped the edge of her pussy, her lips teasingly close to where he touched.

He made eye contact as he cupped her pussy, his firm hold sending a message that his expression confirmed. *This belongs to me. You are mine.*

She nodded, threw her head back, arched onto her elbows and let her knees fall apart so her pussy was on display. *Yours,* her actions confirmed. *Forever and always.*

He hooked her panties with his fingers and yanked them to the side. She held her breath as he moved closer, the heat of his body ironically making her shiver. She lifted a hand to yank her tank top up, exposing her stomach, teasing her fingers higher.

He traced his fingers down her slit, and she jolted, arching up, coaxing him to move closer.

"Ry," she moaned.

She yanked her tank up higher, the built in bra giving way to her breasts with a satisfying release. Her tits tumbled out, and Ry let out a low growl. She wiggled her hips, moving her body so they jiggled.

He growled again and cut her satisfying grin short when he latched onto her clit with his lips. She jolted then froze, not wanting to scare him off, not wanting to stop him from doing what she so badly wanted him to do.

He ran his fingers down her slit again, this time delving in, hunting for her G-spot while he sucked her clit hard enough to shoot stars across her eyes.

She groaned, collapsing, her arms giving out to the pure bliss of Ry touching her.

He licked, flicked, stroked and rubbed.

She brought her hands to her nipples, tweaked, caressed and twisted.

So many sensations swept Elena up. Her heart was full, her body on fire. Her orgasm was a tsunami, back-building, sucking her out to sea and rising, rising, rising until her body burst. Waves of leg-shaking jolts made her pussy quiver and leap. Ry relentlessly continued, pushing her to the point of mind-numbing existence where she couldn't tell where her body was in the universe.

He yanked her up so her head cradled into his shoulder. "Ry," she gasped.

"I know," he said. "But I want more."

He hooked her arms around his shoulders, her limbs limp noodles obeying his commands before her brain caught up to what he was doing.

He hoisted her up his body, coaxing her legs to grip tight as he moved them across the room. He pressed her back against the only bare wall then took her lips, bruising, devouring her, demanding she be present, her mind floating down from the clouds as her body still purred with the remnants of his actions.

She heard the click of his belt coming undone, and her spine tingled. His hand was between them, fumbling with his zipper. She wanted to help but couldn't because her fingers were tangled in his hair, her mouth busy being punished and the thought of him fucking her like an animal made her pussy weep and plead for more.

He grunted as he pulled back, releasing her lips so he could look down into her eyes. His were hooded, dark and stormy. She bit her lip, tilted her chin and met his stare. He nudged his cock at her hole, sending new shivers all over.

"I'll never have enough." His voice was guttural, pained, like he thought he didn't deserve to feel what he was feeling. "I'll want you endlessly."

"Now you know how I feel—have always felt."

Something primal and dangerous flashed over his face. He growled then nuzzled into her throat like he was about to take a bite. He pressed his cock into her pussy like he was worried he'd break her, so she tightened her legs around his waist and pulled his hair, *hard*.

"Fuck me like your soul demands."

He roared, pounding his hips with fury, stretching her wide, driving in deep. He bounced her off the wall, his thrusts so powerful that a painting fell from its hook. He spun her around, continuing to pump her as he walked them to her desk, laying her on her back while he fucked her silly.

He gripped her tits as he rolled his hips, meeting her as she arched, desperately trying to stay put while his pummeling sent her farther and farther up the desk. Things fell off. Something broke. His face was pain and pleasure, bliss caught in the rapture of need.

He noticed her slide, yanked her back by the ankle, then flipped her over so her tits pressed into the wood of her desk and her ass was on display. He pounded her pussy from behind, slapping her ass as hard as he could, leaving marks that she knew would bruise. Nothing felt better. He lifted her by the hips, angling her so he could hit her G-spot, deeper, harder.

His cock was a steel rod, a piston. Her body coiled tight again, on the brink of release as jets of hot cum sprayed her inside and out.

He didn't stop, not even as he roared through his release, not until her pussy quivered for him again, clenching around his cock until she was spent, too.

They collapsed into a sweaty heap on her desk, and she was thankful that she'd gone with the durable oak—strong enough for a fucking, it seemed.

"I wasn't expecting my day to go this way." Elena was laughing with breathless abandon, loving how tangled up they were. His arm was around her back, his head in the crook of her throat. She inhaled his scent, musky and spicy.

"Oh, I was." Ry lifted his head and kissed her softly. "Let me catch my breath, and I'll show you all the ways your day is going to go."

Epilogue

Things were still new between her and Ry, and that meant that every day was an adventure. What she was learning she loved the most was waking up with his arms wrapped around her, his body curled behind her and his soft sleepy voice whispering his love words.

"You're so warm and soft, El. I could stay here all day."

And she wished they could stay in bed, every day, all day.

But she had work and he had...life to live. She'd forced him to take a vacation—to rest, relax, explore New York. There were job offers coming at him all the time, so he could work when he was ready, but for now, she wanted him to live like he'd never allowed himself to.

He made dinner for her every night that they didn't go out. He ran errands and enjoyed it. He loved surprising her at work with lunch and a quickie that left her both satiated and wanting. She couldn't wait to get home. She couldn't wait to get to work. Her life felt full.

She was happy—maybe truly happy for the first time in her life.

This night, though, they had plans, and he wouldn't tell her what they were. She knew he wasn't going anywhere. He'd made it a point to reassure her every day that he was with her for good. Her insecurities had virtually disappeared. But this had vibes of something bigger…something that she'd been dreaming of for a lifetime.

"You want me to wear a blindfold?" She caressed the satin ribbon that was wide enough to cover the top half of her face. "So, it's a whopper of a secret destination, I guess?"

"I do." He kissed her softly as he pulled the fabric from her hand. "And you're to do everything you're told."

A shiver ran down her spine. Her heart thrashed in her chest. She loved surprises. She hated having to wait.

He tied the ribbon tightly, cutting off all light, plunging her into a weird sensory deprivation because she couldn't hear him, couldn't tell if he was even in the same room anymore.

"Some of your friends are here to help you dress." His voice was distant.

"Hey, girl." Cammie's signature tone, all effervescence, came at her like a freight train. "You ready for some fun?"

"I'll see you soon," Ry said, his voice even farther away.

"What is he up to?" Elena said.

"Like we'd tell you," Vivian laughed. "Now turn around. We've got to get you into this dress."

By the rustling, Elena knew before the fabric even touched her skin that she was about to put on a costume of taffeta and crinoline. Her mind flashed back to her eighteenth birthday and the story she'd told the Cats about the escape room games she'd planned. Was Ry recreating that day? Was he pulling her into their shared past? Why? Was he planning a redo?

Certain that she'd figured it all out, she became the most compliant victim to the plans of her friends — pulled, prodded, tugged, tucked. They'd removed her blindfold long enough to do her hair and makeup, somehow without giving her a glimpse of anything below her neck. It felt like an eternity, but finally, once all the fussing had stopped, her friends deemed her worthy.

She still wore a blindfold, this one loose to accommodate her makeup, as they led her to the waiting car — a limo, by the feel of things. Her body was on fire and not because she was nestled in the midst of a lot of fabric but because she was a knot of nerves. What were his plans, exactly? What kind of grand gesture was this going to be? A declaration of love, using those words he'd yet to say out loud to her? Or something else…something more permanent, more committed?

She could barely contain her excitement. She wanted to bounce in the seat. She wanted to scream out of the window. She wanted to peek.

As the car slowed and the temptation grew, she lifted her fingers to her blindfold and slowly nudged the edge.

"Mr. Ward said no peeking, Miss Sasser!" A voice boomed from the front seat.

Elena, feeling chastened, dropped her hand. Heat burned her cheeks, so when the car finally stopped and the door popped open, she knew Ry would see exactly what she'd been up to.

"You're naughty, you know that?" Ry's voice cut through her anxiety. "But I'm proud of you for making it this far."

He helped her out, giant dress and all, then tugged the blindfold free.

Elena blinked a few times. She took in the scene. She was in front of a castle, fit for a princess. "Ry?"

He came around her, standing in a crisp white shirt, obsidian bow tie and tail coat. His hair was slicked to the side, and his jaw was scruffy, just the way she loved. "You're gorgeous," he said.

"So are you!" She closed the distance between them and pressed herself against his body, taking in the scent of old English leather and citrus. "What are you up to?"

He tilted her chin up and kissed her sweetly, leaving her craving more.

"Only what you deserve."

He offered his arm then guided her up the stone steps. "This is the Chateau Ripley, owned by a friend of mine."

She didn't know Ry had friends, but she loved that he did, because the mansion was stunning. It was all sharp edges, immaculate white, stainless steel and windows. Angles jutted, making it look like a haphazard mountain of hovering floors, but the beauty of its architecture wasn't lost on her. It was suspended from the sky, or at least, that's how it looked.

"And this is the beginning of a night you'll never forget."

The entrance was black-and-white marble, more glass, more steel. Everything was shiny, reflecting the colors of her ball gown, which was pink pearl and layered gossamer. It had to have cost him a small fortune, but she loved how soft it was, even with the crinoline brushing against her, the slip that covered her legs silk. He swept her into a ballroom, complete with faux candle dangling glass shard chandeliers and peaked ceilings that jutted this way and that, just like the rest of the house seemed to.

Books lined the walls behind ornate glass and filigree metal work, telling Elena that this doubled as a library when not in use as her and Ry's private dance floor.

Before Elena could dwell on the negativity of the past, Ry led her across the room, her gown sweeping and swaying, making her feel like Belle with her Beast. His eyes were locked into hers, expression serious, so close that she felt his heat, the curl of his fingers on her waist and in her hand. The music came from all sides — waltz music, like the dance she'd learned as a child for her father's fiftieth birthday that she'd never gotten to show him — and her heart felt so full that she was floating.

They danced until they were breathless, until the music quieted, and they slowed enough to speak.

"Time for new memoires," Ry said, a soft smile on his lips.

She grinned, tilting her face up. "I knew that's what you were up to."

He cocked an eyebrow, winked then continued, "Oh, you've got it all figured out, do you?"

His tone made her second guess.

"I would have danced with you that night. I wanted to sweep you up and erase that frown."

"I wish you had." She remembered how dejected she'd felt. She'd been practicing so hard to get the moves right, and her father had known her plans to honor him. His rejection had blown her heart apart. At the time, she'd still had a place for her father in there. She'd covered her embarrassment by saying it was a joke so her friends in attendance wouldn't think she was a loser.

"Thank you for giving me this." It had been a terrible memory that Ry was fixing, so she no longer had to compartmentalize. Now she could let it go and replace it with this one. "Had I known you were watching my humiliation, I would have forced you onto the dance floor."

"That's why I slipped into the crowd, so you didn't know I was there." He laughed. "But I'm here now."

The music started again, a slower song this time, and Ry swept her up all over again.

He'd arranged for a five-course meal, standard procedure when her father was entertaining guests, which was often, and Elena had always been forced to attend.

She had hated how her father always made her feel like she was only there to look at. He'd chastise her for eating too much, while at the same time forcing her to eat things she didn't like. It was a mind game that amused him but had tortured her.

Ry made sure all her favorite foods were present, from oysters and caviar to arugula and apple salad, pasta with vodka sauce to filet mignon with mini potatoes, followed by chocolate mousse.

Every morsel had been selected for her. Every bite of food let her know that Ry had always been paying attention. It sent shivers over her body to be at the center of his focus, to recognize that he always saw her, even when she thought she was invisible to him.

When dinner was through, he led her to the den where a huge fireplace roared with flames. In front of it was a tumble of comforters, a little nest for them.

Not exactly like the fireplace at the resort but close enough.

He got down on one knee and looked up at her through hooded eyes.

Elena held her breath as her hand fluttered to her throat.

"Elena, I've wanted to make a night of memories that should have happened a long time ago for us. I wanted to show you that I was always in love with you, even when I was pretending not to be." He opened a box and inside was a princess-cut emerald, nestled in gold, just as she'd always wanted. "Elena, I want to be with you forever and make up for lost time. Will you marry me?"

Elena dropped to her knees and cupped his face. Tears slipped from her eyes, unbidden.

"I've been waiting forever for you to say those words." She kissed him with all her love.

"Is that a yes?" he asked as she pulled away.

"Of course, it is!" She held out her hand, and the moment the ring slid on, she felt like every day forward would be her happiest.

Then with the utmost gentleness, he helped her shed her clothing. The dress was easy, and Ry held her gaze as he unzipped her from the base of her neck to the dip of her ass. He coaxed the top from her shoulders, releasing her breasts so the fabric pooled at her waist.

"You make me happier than I've ever been," he said, his voice rough, his eyes stormy.

He kissed her gently, lingering for a half second before leaning his forehead against hers.

"My heart is full, too," Elena said.

He lifted her with little effort, holding her by the waist and taking her out of the ripples of fabric around her. When he laid her down on the cushioned floor, she felt the heat of his gaze roam her body as he slipped the rest of her undergarments off.

With a ring on her finger and nothing else, Ry lay with her in front of fire, wrapping his arms around her as he caressed her body and opened her soul. He entwined his tongue with hers and made her scream his name. He filled her up and completed her heart.

Finally, finally they were together — forever, for always.

Want to see more from this author? Here's a taster for you to enjoy!

Hell Hath No Fury: Scorned
Angela Addams

Excerpt

"Are we going to get some street meat or what?" Ruby gleefully shouted as she slung one arm out, pointing her finger in the direction of sustenance.

"Hang on, friend. I need to grab some cash." I tugged Ruby's other arm toward a side street where the bright glow of an ATM beckoned me.

It was late—or early, depending on what side of the moon you were on. Two a.m. and greasy sausages from the vendor down the road was top priority after a night of tequila shots.

Ruby was tanked, and I was feeling a nice floaty buzz, which gave me a perma-smile that hurt my cheeks and made my lips ache.

"Maybe I'll crash at your place tonight," Ruby slurred as she slumped against the wall next to the ATM, her body like a limp noodle. "Take a vacay from my life."

The city streets were wafting some pretty heavy heat after the scorcher of the last few days. Summer was dying, and we were all paying for it. The patios had been full when we'd gone to grab dinner earlier, and the bars had been packed when we'd done a bit of hopping from one dive to the next. It had been fun, but I reeked of other people's sweat, and I was ready to go home.

"My place is hardly a vacation destination." *Understatement of the century.*

My place was a dump, with its hundred-year-old cracked plaster, peeling wallpaper and rusty pipes. But it was *my* dump, and I had been lucky to find something in the heart of Toronto. I got what Ruby was craving, though — peace, solitude, time away from her boyfriend's two kids under five and her boyfriend, who might as well be kid number three. She wanted to stretch out her night of freedom, sleep until late in the morning. drink coffee that she didn't have to chug and maybe have a bagel and some eggs that she didn't have to eat cold. "I can't promise you five-star anything, but you know my couch is always yours."

"I love your place. It's got so much old-world charm." Ruby hiccupped as she rolled her head toward me, a silly grin making her eyes light up. "What's taking so long? There's a big fat juicy sausage calling to me."

"That's so dirty." I attempted to joke, even though I was frowning at the machine, which had rejected my passcode twice already. "Don't know." I punched my code in a third time then slammed my hand against the side of the machine, because violence was always just under the surface for me. "What the fuck?"

"Here… Let me use my card." Ruby pushed off the wall. "Move out of the way."

"I can't." I was rooted in place. My feet stuck as I stared at the machine that was telling me my bank account didn't exist. *It doesn't exist?* "It won't give my card back."

I punched some buttons, agitation quickly turning to frantic rage. I had money in there. My monthly 'shut up and disappear' money would have gone in at midnight, replenishing the joint account with what I was owed. I slammed my open palm against the panel again, and the sting reverberated up my arm.

"Whoa there, lady." A smooth voice slid out of the darkness, dripping with bad intentions. "That machine ain't done nothing wrong." He stepped too close to Ruby, pulling my attention away from the ATM.

Ruby's eyes went wide. She straightened her back and winced. "Charlie." My name was a squeak that shuddered past her lips. A tremor shook her shoulders.

The hairs on the back of my neck perked up.

He was wearing a gray hoodie pulled up over his scraggly dark hair. That and the shadow shielding his face made it impossible to get a good look at him. "You ladies are going to give me what you've got in your bank accounts." He nudged Ruby, and she opened her mouth like she was going to scream, but he clamped his hand over her face. "Quietly."

A loser holding up two women. *Classy.*

"I can't give you jack," I said with a nod to the machine, which was now flashing a recommendation to call my bank. "This piece of shit just ate my card." He didn't need to know about my other bank account.

He snorted what sounded like a laugh, and I got a waft of something not quite right. I mean, aside from the fact that he was trying to rob us, there was also a jitter about him that was making me think he was tweaked out on something. That, or he was really, really on edge. "I'm taking payment one way or the other."

It was obvious that he had a weapon wedged against Ruby's back by the way she was arching her spine. I didn't know if he was hurting her or if it was fear, but she was contorting as far away as she could get with his hand on her mouth. "You scream, and I hurt you. Got it?"

Ruby nodded as tears spilled down her cheeks.

He lifted his meaty hand away. "You try your card."

She made a mumbly noise then staggered toward me, towing the guy along with her.

I didn't know if he had a gun or knife or if he was just using his fingers to scare the hell out of Ruby, but his eyes were dark and menacing, his pupils pinpricks. He licked his chapped lips as he gave me a once-over. I felt dirty just from his gaze. When he met my eyes again and his lips curled into a smug grin, I knew he wasn't bluffing. The guy liked to make women scream.

I calculated the odds of Ruby getting hurt if I took action.

He was taller than me by at least a foot. Heavier, too. Probably had about a hundred pounds on me, maybe more. He likely had a weapon—cowards like him always did. I'd handled bigger men than him. I'd taken down meaner ones, too. I could deal with a bullet, even a few bullets. Nobody used silver anymore and lead, steel and brass are practically mosquito bites. Stab wounds? They would close with time.

"You do anything stupid, and I'll kill her," he growled like he was reading my mind.

It wasn't me who would get hurt. Ruby was a fragile human—and not just physically. She was riding high on adrenaline right now, but that would crash soon, then she'd go into shock.

She was shaking as she frantically dug into her bag, presumably for her bank card. She was sucking air into her mouth and barely letting any go. Her fear was a rising tide, and she was going to drown.

I lifted my hands—the universal sign for surrender—and took a step back to make room for Ruby in front of the machine.

"I c-c-can't find my c-c-card."

Like a snake, the guy struck, smacking Ruby up the side of her head then threading his fingers into her hair. He pushed her head down toward her chest and shoved her closer to the machine. She choked on a sob.

"Stop fucking around," the thief growled.

My hackles were up, flooding high-octane rage into my muscles. My body bulked. I rolled my shoulders back, cracked my spine, narrowed my eyes and did everything I could to keep the beast inside me under control. If she came out, this guy was going to die, and I didn't want to have to explain that to anyone. "Take your hands off her."

He skittered his gaze to me, tilting his head like I was intriguing him—like he found me amusing. "You ain't calling the shots here, lady."

"I found it!" Ruby whipped her card out but couldn't seem to coordinate herself to slide it into the slot.

I clenched and unclenched my fists, tightening my jaw so my molars were grinding. The tingle of anticipation made my gums burn and my fingers ache.

Keep it steady, Charlie.

For Ruby's sake, I was fighting the primal urge to lash out. If I hurt him, he'd hurt her. I needed to bide my time. Wait him out. He'd make a mistake. They always did.

When she failed to get the card into the slot on her third try, he tightened his grip in her hair. "I said, stop fucking around."

"I'm sorry!" She managed to shove the card in, then worked on punching her code on the keypad. "I can only take out five hundred."

"Fuck," he muttered as he speared me with another disgusting once-over. "I guess that means you two are coming with me for the night." As if that hadn't always been his plan.

We waited as the machine whirred then spit out a wad of cash. He was practically salivating at the sight of it. He let go of Ruby's hair then reached for the money at the same time that I curled my fingers over Ruby's wrist to yank her behind me. The sudden movement startled him. He lifted his weapon.

Not a gun.

One badass-looking knife, though.

"Run," I ordered Ruby as I leapt to block the guy from her. He lunged, and I swiped his face, my fist connecting with a rock-hard jaw and sending bolts of pain up my arm.

"Ow, you bitch!" He swung his curved blade down, reaching out to get a hold of my hair, but I ducked and weaved, nailing him in the side with another punch. This time my fist sank in, missing his ribs altogether, drilling him in the liver instead—or trying to, anyway. The guy was made of marbled meat.

He groaned but not surprisingly, didn't go down. I ducked again when he tried to slam me with his blade but miscalculated his reflexes and took an uppercut to the chin. It sent me reeling backward, lights flashing across my vision.

Ouch.

As I was shaking it off, Ruby screamed. The guy pivoted in her direction.

Fuck.

I'd told her to run, but instead, she was frozen like prey.

I leapt onto this back and wrapped my arm around his thick neck. My fingers, complete with partially distended claws against his jugular, were hidden by his hood.

Blending in meant being subtle with my abilities — for both self-preservation and to avoid unwanted attention. I'd had three years to master my partial shift and was proud to say that Ruby had no idea her best friend was a werewolf.

"Take one more step, and I'll bleed you like a pig," I snarled against his ear. To punctuate my threat, I let my claws poke into his skin, drawing first blood. The smell of it revved me up, making my wolf want to howl and my beast want to rip his throat out. I tightened my hold and leveraged myself closer, clamping down on my predatory urges. My fangs dropped, burning through my gums. I scraped them along his jaw and took pleasure in his whimper. "One twitch and you're dead." My voice was guttural, filled with malice that I knew he understood.

The acrid smell of piss hit my nose. *Oh, how the tables have turned.*

"Drop the knife," I ordered.

It clattered to the ground.

I urged my fangs to slink back into my gums but kept the pressure on his throat with my claws. "Ruby, call the cops."

But really, what this guy needed was a good scare and some beastly tough love.

* * * *

We were at the hospital so Ruby could get checked out. She was obviously in shock, with glassy eyes, mumbling a confusing account of what went down. The police had taken our statements already, but it was mine that made sense, so it was mine that would go into their report, which was better for everyone.

I snuck away while the doctor was checking Ruby out and made a call.

"Well, if it isn't the bitch of the hour," Vince drawled, wide awake at holy fuck in the morning, as usual. "To what do I owe this honor, Charlotte?"

"What the fuck did you do to my bank account?" I growled. Attempted robbery aside, finding out that my money was gone had ruined my night. "Where's my cash, asshole?"

"Whoa, whoa, whoa!" Vince sucked on something, probably a fat cigar, then blew into the phone. "You're acting like I'm the one messing up your life, when really, that's all on you, babe."

"I have a contract and a clan vow. First of the month, money goes into that account." I never wanted the account to be joint, but my stepbrother, Andy, had insisted that it must be that way for the family to agree to the deal. I always transferred it at the stroke of midnight to my own personal account anyway, but tonight I had plans and didn't think it would be a big deal to do it a little later than normal. That, apparently, had been a miscalculation on my part.

"Contract and vow are void," Vince said, like I should already know. "Andy isn't in charge anymore. You are S.O.L."

Whatever was left in my gut bottomed out, and I was suddenly nauseous. "Did they kill him?" That was the only way Andy would step down from being alpha of the clan. "What happened?"

I wasn't going to pretend that I was on any type of lovey-dovey terms with my stepbrothers, but Andy was less of a dick than the rest of them. When he'd taken over running the clan after my dad had passed, he'd struck a deal with me to disappear. I had, happily, and for the last three years, he'd upheld his end of it with a monthly stipend delivered wirelessly at the stroke of midnight.

"He's not dead. He's just…incapacitated."

Fuck! Fuckfuckfuckfuck.

"Where is he?"

"That's privileged information, sweetheart." Vince grunted.

"Who's alpha? Del? Lucas?" Either one of my shithead stepbrothers would run the clan into the ground. Both were vindictive enough to shut my account down and void our agreement.

"You've got it all wrong, babe. Sal is alpha now. And it would be a good idea for you to pay your respects…*in person.*"

"Sal?" *Holy fuck!* "He was ousted." My father had kicked him out when he'd gone on a rampage, blood-raging all over Vancouver Island, and had killed a bunch of tourists on a nature hike. I remembered the day my father had sat us all down at the house and told us our brother, my stepbrother, was ex-communicated. Removal from the clan was the ultimate slap in the face. More than that, it was a walking death sentence to be a wolf with no clan affiliation, and it was supposed to be permanent.

"Lone wolf is back and…sweetie? He's not too happy with you and the arrangement you weaseled out of dear old Andrew."

Yeah, because a guy like that would rather have me barefoot and pumping out little werewolf babies than having a life of my own on my own terms. 'Independent female werewolf' was not in his vocabulary. We only existed to serve men like him.

Plus, if my uncle had blabbed about my werebeast, then Sal was probably hungry for a demonstration. Not many females could turn into deformed monsters like I could.

I was special that way.

"I had a sanctioned deal," I spat, rage burning through my brain until all I could see were flames. *That motherfucker!* I kicked a garbage can, which drew the attention of a security guard, who swiveled in my direction.

"I tell you what, *Charlie*," Vince snarled. "Sal will be at the head office tomorrow. I can pencil you in for a meeting so you can discuss your displeasure with the management of *his* funds. I'll even buy you a ticket to get here."

I closed my eyes, took a deep breath then blew it out. When I opened my eyes, the guard was still looking at me but hadn't come any closer. I turned my back on him as I exited the hospital. "Yeah, fine, book me a ticket, asshole." I hung up before he could reply.

The best way to deal with a dictator like Sal was to get right up in his face, and that was what I planned to do. He didn't know it yet, but he was about to meet a side of me he couldn't control.

About the Author

Angela Addams is an author of many naughty things. She believes that the written word is an amazing tool for crafting the most erotic of scenarios and likes telling stories about normal people getting down and dirty and falling in love. Enthralled by the paranormal at an early age, Angela also spends a lot of her time thinking up new story ideas that involve supernatural creatures in everyday situations.

She is an avid tattoo collector, a total book hoarder, and loves anything covered in chocolate…except for bugs.

She lives in Ontario, Canada in an old, creaky house, with her husband, children and four moody cats.

Angela loves to hear from readers. You can find her contact information, website details and author profile page at https://www.totallybound.com

Home of Erotic Romance

Sign up for our newsletter and find out about all our romance book releases, eBook sales and promotions, sneak peeks and FREE romance books!